Erich Wolfgang Skwara

Black Sails

Translated by Derk Wynand

ARIADNE PRESS
Riverside, California

Ariadne Press would like to express its appreciation to the Austrian Cultural Institute, New York, and the Bundeskanzleramt, Sektion Kunst, Vienna for assistance in publishing this book.

Translated from the German
Schwarze Segelschiffe
claassen Verlag Düsseldorf, 1979
© Erich Wolfgang Skwara

Library of Congress Cataloging-in-Publication Data

Skwara, Erich Wolfgang, 1948-
 [Schwarze Segelschiffe. English]
 Black sails / Erich Wolfgang Skwara : translated by Derk Wynand.
    p.   cm. -- (Studies in Austrian literature, culture, and thought. Translation Series.)
 ISBN 1-57241-069-8
 I. Wynand, Derk. II. Title. III. Series.
 PT2681.K8S3913 1999
 833'.*14--dc21   98-48468
                                                              CIP

Cover design:
Art Director and Designer: George McGinnis

Copyright ©1999
by Ariadne Press
270 Goins Court
Riverside, CA 92507

All rights reserved.
No part of this publication may be reproduced or transmitted in any form or by any means without formal permission.
Printed in the United States of America.
ISBN 1-57241-069-8
(Paperback original)

"Vous n'avez pas commis une mauvaise action, vous avez commis un délit."

Henry de Montherlant ("Tous feux éteints")

1

"I am the director," the director said, "and I'll determine your positions. Your actions are your own; you're free. I don't care about that, so long as you respond if I burst into your lives with a shout of: No, not like that, again! I'm the director. Never forget that."

The director sat up and looked at the circle of his guests. He could have called these few people gathered around him his friends but preferred to think of them as guests. After all he had summoned them – yet again – for the sole purpose of drumming into their heads that he and he alone was the director. Once a month or more he brought them together on some pretext or other to remind them of his directorial function. These assemblies always proved embarrassing.

The pride in his eyes lent them an unbecoming darkness. The pupils were darkened like silver chains that can blacken within hours around an invalid's neck.

He drank a great deal, several bottles a day, though never anything but wine. Now he was drunk again and when drunk he needed company. Thus the gatherings, during which the guests were reminded and admonished, actually served a dual purpose.

In exile, too, the director surrounded himself with people he called actors even if they were not. Many years ago he had left his native land, Germany, and the city of Munich, never to return, not even for an hour. But because he could have driven there at any time it seemed a ridiculous exile.

Back home he had not been exactly famous – directorial concepts like literary or musical ones frequently go unappreciated – and in his exile he was generally unemployed. Though he had spent years in France, he hardly spoke any French. Thus Paris was passing him by. He knew it and it pained him, but that is just what he wanted.

What the director lacked most was important professional contacts. He was lacking in everything a man needs to get ahead. But does someone not getting ahead make less progress as a result?

He was not a handsome man. Sitting at a table he resembled a crouching wicked gnome, and yet he could make an impression. He was splendidly articulate, gifted with an admirable voice, but he would give recitations only on solitary walks through a deserted park. Mostly he kept silent. For all that he perfected daily the art of direction, which can be mute as everyone knows. Wherever he went, inside or out, even in his own almost bare flat, he directed.

Whenever something occurred that did not fit the general design, those involved twaddled about coincidence, even about fate. Such talk depressed the director. No one else seemed to understand that the best directing must of necessity be cruel and invisible as well.

To earn a living he worked as a guide. He would sit in a large tour bus, pick up the microphone and expound on the city of Paris to some tourists or other. Every morning he would thus divide the city of exile into new dimensions and categories. No two groups ever heard the same thing. The director had the metropolis of Paris itself at his disposal.

Then Tristan ran into the room, breathlessly shouting, "The actress is coming!"

Everyone turned briefly to the shouting man, all thinking the actress was about to enter the room that very second. But only Tristan entered, hesitating in the doorway. For weeks he had raved about this actress until the others found him tiresome. All the while no one knew *which* actress he was talking about. Tristan did not mention her name but spoke only of *the actress*, each time stressing the word voluptously.

She was to come from Munich, where the director had once also lived. There, years ago, Tristan had been in love with her. At the time the two had childishly resolved to live together, but then his restlessness had driven him to other parts of the world and the two lost sight of each other. They had not seen each other since nor exchanged any letters. Only when Tristan had returned to Paris and met the director there had he remembered the actress again. Inconceivably for him, memory had soon changed to desire. He had shaken his head in surprise at himself when he finally went to phone her after so many years.

"It's odd how you can be reached at any hour," Tristan had said to the startled woman. "You can always be found in the same place, at the same number, as if all of you did nothing but wait. I find that both splendid and terrible."

The actress was astonished by such a greeting and by his use of the plural, but she could come up with no fitting response. And when Tristan finally invited her to Paris, she accepted without hesitation. He sent her the plane ticket the very next day. But she had some engagements, the flight had to be postponed, there were further phone calls that did not however shed any light on the point of the journey. And she wondered why Tristan had not sent a return ticket, but did not give it much thought. She had never been to Paris and did not know whether she had accepted for the city's sake or

Tristan's.

"The actress is coming!" He repeated as he went into the room. There was no seat for him and this irritated him, Tristan, for whom everything, even joy, turned to sorrow. From this ludicrous circumstance he immediately deduced a great hostility on the part of people and things, and he regretted having said, "The actress is coming." He blushed in embarrassment. The director's guests were still staring his way, even though he had long been standing in their midst.

The word "actress" was like a cue for the drunken director. Lost in thought these last weeks, he had taken no note of Tristan's words, though the actress had already been under discussion for a long time. "If an actress is coming," he said, "then it's up to me to determine her entrance. No matter whom she's coming to visit, I am the director!" He got up and went to the door, assuming she would enter at any moment.

"No!" Tristan said. "The actress is still in Munich. She's boarding the plane at this very moment. So I still have thirty minutes. Then I'll drive to the airport to pick her up."

"And I will go along," the director said. "You, sad Tristan, and I, the director – we'll pick the actress up together, together we'll capture her . . ."

Unable to decide whether this prospect left him indifferent or annoyed, Tristan did not resist the decision. "Fine, so we'll pick her up together."

In the cab they were amazed how simple it was, with a bit of money, to transform the destinies of strangers into their own. "Basically, every occupation is a despicable form of prostitution," Tristan said. "But actors are the worst: they sell not only their time and goals, but also their feelings –

since a good actor does not act out his feelings, but lives them. We're driving to the airport to pick up a whore. We're letting a foreign whore into Paris, which is teeming with beautiful whores."

"The best actor is also the vilest person," the director replied, "but it's much the same for most callings. I'm one of the most significant directors; my punishment is to be unemployed."

As the cab approached the airport Tristan grew increasingly nervous. The director's features sharpened so that he reminded Tristan of a lurking spider. "I haven't bought a return ticket for the actress yet," he said casually.

Bored, the director said, "That's good, for she won't be needing one."

The two remained silent. Then Tristan, visibly agitated, said, "Maybe I won't recognize her. It's been years since I saw her last."

"An actor, an actress," the director said, "can always be recognized on the spot. You don't want to recognize these people, but you do so at once."

"But what do I do if she's become ugly in the meantime? I can't stand ugly people," Tristan said.

"Unlike other people, an actor cannot become ugly," the director said. "At all events, an actor is useful."

The cab stopped; they had reached the terminal. Once Tristan had paid the driver, who then drove off in his empty cab, he envied him for being able to simply depart and not deal with the actress. He would have preferred to slip into the cabdriver's skin. The director on the other hand seemed pleased and impatient. He entered the terminal ahead of Tristan and shouted to him from some distance, "The plane from

Munich has landed!" When Tristan caught up with him, he grasped the still reluctant man by the arm and pulled him to the automatic glass door through which all arrivals left customs. "So many people are waiting here," the director said, tightening his grip on Tristan's arm, "and strictly speaking, they're all waiting for *their* actor."

"I'm only waiting for my actress, and for me the others are anything but stage people," Tristan replied.

"You can enjoy the luxury of mental reduction because you're not the director," the director said, "but in fact not even you should indulge in such luxury. It could prove dangerous for you someday. It's your attitude above all that renders directing inaccessible to you."

They had been speaking animatedly and too loud. Others were staring at them in disapproval. But perhaps the German language had stirred displeasure. "One shouldn't speak German in public, especially not too loud," Tristan said. After that they kept silent and stared at the glass door through which the first arrivals were now passing. But the actress was not among these speedier ones, as they had hoped.

"The disillusionment is already starting," Tristan reflected, not voicing the thought. Without a word, the director suddenly left the waiting crowd and crossed the enormous terminal until he had reached its most deserted part. Tristan followed him with his eyes. The director let himself fall into a black vinyl armchair at the end of the hall and collapsed. Tristan again thought the man resembled a spider, even at such a distance. The conviction that he was dealing not with a director, not with a human being but with a spider, became so paramount for him that he could finally restrain himself no longer and, ignoring the crowds in the arrivals hall, he shouted at the top of his lungs, "You spider!"

Those waiting and the arrivals were electrified by this shout that here in France surely no one understood. All cringed for a split second, looked at Tristan, then sought the man for whom the shout had been intended and finally shook their heads in amusement or indignation. This symmetry of shaking heads amazed Tristan. "A veritable puppet show," he thought, but his thoughts were cut short by the resounding laughter his shouting had provoked in the director. The latter was not ashamed to spew out a madman's laughter, loud, filling the large terminal. Instead of stopping, his laughter intensified outrageously. Again several bystanders were indignant; others joined in the laughter. From the far end of the hall the director's madness determined everything.

Then the actress appeared through the sliding glass door.

"The actress is here!" Tristan called in a loud voice.

But the director did not seem to hear. He laughed and laughed, and so it happened that the actress, who had imagined herself in Paris, did not so much enter the city as step into the laughter, a thing she obviously took personally, for she stopped, blushing, in her tracks.

Her hair was dyed a reddish shade. In the years since Tristan had been in love with her she had put on weight without being fat. She was painfully conscious of every detail in her life, and her greatest fear was ridicule. She took all the world's laughter personally, which the director was later to describe as insolent. "Not all laughter pertains to you, my child. My laughter certainly doesn't pertain to you, but to me."

Tristan approached and greeted her, kissing her awkwardly on the left cheek and, reluctantly, on the right as well. The bystanders were sufficiently distracted by their own waiting or by the director's laughter not to regard Tristan and his failed attempts at kissing, yet he was embarrassed by his intimacies with the actress. Because he was bound to sorrow, the most superficial gestures, meaningless to others, became the most cumbersome intimacies for him. He sensed that he no longer loved or desired her, that she disgusted him in fact. Even in her he was seeking his past, and whoever finds that is of course disappointed. The actress, mere history, had become the present again. "I can't get out of it. For two or three days I'll have to be nice to this creature," Tristan thought.

"We've both changed," he told her then. "We'll have to get used to each other again. At least it will give our boring lives a purpose."

"But my life's not boring," said the actress in whose voice Tristan thought he could hear all Germany speaking.

"Don't contradict me!" he yelled at the newly arrived woman with a furious resolve he would not have thought himself capable of and, softer if not softly, he added, "Good of you to come."

She was stunned. Tristan, on the other hand, ascertained that human encounters were increasingly difficult for him. "Come," he said to her. "Let me introduce you to the director. I didn't come to the airport alone. I've brought the director along."

She stopped, uncomprehending. "But this is a private visit. Am I here on business now?"

"We always consider ourselves private, but we never are." He led the confused actress to the director. As they made their way across the terminal, Tristan felt ashamed of her.

In fact he had been ashamed of her all along. He made a distinction between friendships he could reveal openly and those that were to remain private. He appeared in public only with the most beautiful people, yet he sometimes loved the less beautiful all the more ardently. But whatever befell him became devalued, turning to memory even as it was experienced.

"This is the director," Tristan told the actress. "And this is the actress." With an exaggerated wave of the hand he introduced her to the still laughing man. She tried to oblige with a smile, but in vain, because she was blushing deeply once more. The director remained seated in the black vinyl chair and laughed, uttering his words amid laughter. "This is the actress, so this is the actress, this really is the actress?"

She did not know how to conduct herself. Tristan did not help her out of her predicament, but stood aloof from the blushing and the laughter.

Meanwhile all the travelers had been dispatched, no further planes had arrived and the enormous hall of glass and artificial marble was nearly deserted now. But the director's directorial concept had inconspicuously passed over into Tristan, and it seemed that three people had remained in the hall. An outside observer would identify two men and a woman speaking German, but outside reports carry little weight.

2

The actress lay stretching on her bed when Tristan and the director entered her room. Their large bodies made her blood run cold. She lay helpless before these upright men. She felt like a snake but, unable to hiss and strike, she curled up under the blankets and pretended to sleep. But Tristan would not be fooled. He sat heavily on her bed. "You're neither rehearsing nor making an appearance now, so don't put on an act! We've seen your open eyes."

At that the actress knew she would not escape the two. She sat up and tried to smile. "I don't want to be up and starting the day," she said, "for no sooner do I get out of bed than I stumble on the words and phrases you set in my way. If I lie here, on the other hand, then I offer no resistance to these phrases and they pour over me. Please let me sleep. . ."

"No," the director replied firmly, not having said anything so far this morning, "we cannot and will not spare you a thing. Now do get up." He pulled the blankets from her.

Though wearing blue pajamas, she felt embarrassed, but more out of convention than genuine shame. When she found neither of them bothering to look at her, she felt offended. "My body's appealing after all," she thought, while at the same time wondering whether she really was. For seconds she was totally absorbed in herself and forgot the two men.

But Tristan called himself and the director back into her consciousness. "We know just what you're thinking," he said. "Must you be just like other women?"

She felt humiliated and hurt by these words. In a cold

voice, she asked, "Well then, you clever pair, how might that be?"

Tristan bent over the recumbent woman and gazed with pity into her eyes. "You were embarrassed when the director pulled the blanket away, but you immediately thought: Here I lie in my snug pajamas, exposed to the gaze of these two men and that's sure to arouse them, and so I'm the stronger again." He stared unblinking into the eyes of the actress, who tried vainly to meet his gaze. Even before he had finished his sentence, she had turned away and quietly cursed the blameless day.

"But I only came to Paris," she said, "to see you again. I wasn't prepared to meet nor am I interested in meeting your friends, and I didn't expect to be living alone in a hotel room. Both of you do have flats in the city. Why did you put me up in a hotel and then move into the hotel yourselves? Am I not good enough to visit your places? It's been eighteen hours since I arrived in Paris, but I haven't seen anything of the city. You're keeping me in this hotel like a prisoner. If you don't show me the city today I'm flying back to Munich tonight." She had talked a lot and ever more rapidly and now she was exhausted.

"On first impression," the director said, "one might declare the actress's complaints sound and justified. But if one listens more closely, as I've done from time to time, then the actress is wrong all the same."

"I couldn't care less what you have to say! Tristan, I want you all to myself. Now send the director away!" Her voice broke slightly.

Tristan began stroking her bare forearms in totally unerotic fashion. "Things just aren't that simple, my dear," he said, soft but firm. "We must keep our composure. Look, we've checked you and ourselves into this exclusive hotel so we can be together in style, and we're meeting in a city that offers no basis for German thoughts. Since you were born, you've lived in a country with a system of self-deception, and we want to and must liberate you from this system. You'll understand that I can't send the director away, for without direction we'd all end up in chaos. So calm down and be glad not to hear empty compliments for once. How extraordinary no longer to be a woman but a creature of the stage."

"Stage characters are always neutral," the director added, as he too sat down on the bed of the actress, who was now quite surrounded.

"Why *must* you free me from my 'system,' as you call it?" she asked stubbornly. "Who says I want to be changed?"

"I've slept with you," Tristan replied, placing his syllables deliberately, "and soon after I left your system. I learned – and the realization was painful – that I could not live with a woman from your country in my present life and probably not in my future. The very idea's absurd, a bit like planting icebergs. At the airport I told you we'd have to get used to each other again. But since I've pulled ahead of you in the meantime, I naturally can't lower myself to your level. Rather you'll have to climb up to mine, and Paris will be this exaltation. So don't be defensive, but *calm*. We too will be infinitely calm with you, even if you do cower and cringe."

"You speak as if in a trance," the actress said, "and you're not a little conceited. Who told you that these few nights together meant so much to me? I was very young at the time, impressionable, but I've met lots of other men since."

"That's not the point," the director said, distressed. "We don't want to belittle, but exalt one another. So be still, actress. If anyone must speak German, then let him redeem himself by speaking softly."

She said nothing.

Tristan looked sad. "It's grown so quiet around me," he said, "that I'm afraid of myself. Tell me," he said to the actress, "do you really want to fly home or would you like to spend these three short days with me?"

"I'd like to be with you." She was surprised how easily the decision came.

Suddenly an ethereal silence filled the room. Each of the three felt it, and not even the director denied it afterwards.

"We should have persisted in our immobility for all time," he conceded to Tristan and the actress hours later, "but it wouldn't have fit into my concept. In the long run direction's impossible without movement."

"But why can't you give up directing?" Tristan had asked then, but the director did not answer.

"Come, we'll give the actress time to get dressed and then we'll go down to breakfast," Tristan suggested, breaking the silence.

"Now you've spoiled the lovely silence," the actress said with a smile. All at once she felt relaxed and hardly conscious of her body.

Tristan found her beautiful so long as she wore no makeup. "Stay as you are," he said therefore and realized how foolish the suggestion was.

The elevator that carried Tristan, the actress and the director down to breakfast stopped at nearly every floor.

Sometimes a person got in and sometimes there was no one, the seconds-long delay serving no purpose. But when someone did step into the elevator Tristan held his breath, as if unable to breathe in the presence of strangers, and was seized with anxiety. The actress took his arm. "Don't you feel well?"

"Sure, great," he answered. "I'm just a bit claustrophobic."

"Don't I have a sharp eye?" the actress asked the director, who had not said a word for some time. But he remained silent, and only when Tristan urged him not to be so sullen did he hiss, "You manikins!"

Then they had reached the ground floor and stepped out of the elevator.

"For me breakfast is the most important pillar of the day. Even when I go to sleep at night I'm already looking forward to breakfast, for which I always allow plenty of time," the actress said in the restaurant where they sat at a window table bathed in light.

"I, on the other hand, almost always skip breakfast," Tristan replied. "Mornings my daily and lifelong process of poor planning and omissions begins."

The waiter brought ham and eggs, bread, butter, jam and honey, hot chocolate, coffee and orange juice.

"It strikes me as significant," the director said, "that the actress enjoys breakfast. But how could such a colorful and fragrant affair like this lovely breakfast really mean anything to us? Today's an exception: we'll take the time to have breakfast with the actress. But it's a superficial exception, a back-drop as it were, for she relishes her breakfast. We only wolf it down."

"How can anyone have such bitter thoughts when the sun's shining?" the actress teased. Her sentence did not have the desired effect on the director, and even Tristan's mood seemed to darken.

"We too love the sun," he said, "but do we have the right?"

She thought this talk was going too far. "Enough of this twaddle about right and wrong," she said, "when it's a question of simple and natural things like the sun!"

Tristan and the director exchanged glances and nods. "Yes, for an actress the sun is as much a matter-of-course as are the parts she plays. It can be seen in any theater." The director's voice grew louder. "Why exactly did I leave Germany? Why did I take flight from that terrible country? Because the actors no longer wrap themselves in the souls of their parts, because they don't even want to know who Medea is, Ophelia, Lady Macbeth Gretchen, because they slip their own tiny dimensions over these great personages. Medea, Ophelia, Lady Macbeth are no longer Medea, Ophelia, Lady Macbeth, but are turned into a minor actress who comes to Paris on a visit and understands nothing!" The director shouted the last words so loudly that the restaurant's patrons looked toward the table of the threesome.

"Are you trying to insult me?" the actress asked, her youth working against the desired sharpness of intonation.

"I wish I knew how," the director said.

"Your ham and eggs will get cold," Tristan said, and the director and actress really did keep quiet for a while, listlessly prodding the food with their forks. Meanwhile the sun advanced toward noon and the director suddenly found himself singled out by a most radiant light. From their now shadowy ends of the table, Tristan and the actress could marvel at the sunlight, strictly circumscribed beams in which myriads of dust particles were dancing. But the director sat blinded, grotesquely shading his eyes with his right arm.

"Now you've even been chosen to sit in the sun," Tristan said calmly, "but the chosen must submit to being blinded a little."

Because of the light the actress had forgotten the director's insults. She turned to him but remained in the shade. "Be happy," she said, and the director, surprised and blinded, sat quite helpless. "I am happy."

"If we're not true to human beings," Tristan mused aloud, "then why can't we be true to joy? At least we shouldn't show this most fickle of emotions the door. Director, be happy for more than a few minutes at a time!"

"And boredom?" the director asked in turn. "I am after all responsible for variety."

"Once again I don't understand a thing," the actress said. "Human beings can be held by the hair or arms and they don't keep disappearing when you sit at the same table with them. But you two – you're like phantoms. What are you playing at?"

"You don't understand the art of interrogation, *little actress*," Tristan said very softly. "You're asking forbidden questions."

"Don't call me *little actress*," the actress said, and Tristan replied, "Fine, I won't call you *little actress*. There, you see, I'm being good, I'm obeying you."

"I don't see any connections in what you two are saying," she said. "True, I can see you're not malicious basically, but your sweetness strikes me as uncanny. It isn't natural, it's sick. With you," she repeated softly, "where are the connections?"

"Whoever claims to know connections," the director said in a low voice, "has patched them together with glue. He's a liar."

Having spilled coffee on the tablecloth with a clumsy movement, the actress tapped her fingers on the tabletop. "What I really don't know with either of you," she continued, "is where I stand, whether you're taking me seriously or making fun of me."

"Even that question has no answer," Tristan interrupted her. "The issue is something else entirely and my name obliges me to think about it. – You're certainly a highly gifted actress, but how did you become so gifted and how will you remain so or not? Don't you see that it's more than a question of rank and position, of our dwarfish part in this gigantic world? Don't you understand that I summoned you, the actress, to Paris in order to exalt you, the girlfriend, according to the age-old principle? In the days ahead we'll have to go for many walks. And the director is no betrayal of our private encounter, dear actress. He's simply there and I can't send him away. Can you send him away? Could anyone show the director the door? I don't know."

Tristan had addressed her more and more quickly and passionately. Now he was paler than before and the sweat appeared on his brow. "I've babbled myself into quite a state," he said after a pause and again he blushed.

"You're behaving like a little boy." Happily, the actress closed her hands, clamlike, around his right hand.

The director, who had watched in silence, laughed in dismay.

"Why are you laughing?" Tristan asked and he answered, "I'm laughing at the arrogant realization that my every thought is more original than the thoughts of others. I'm enjoying my renewed confidence that pulls my skin taut and turns it to marble."

They all fell silent.

Reluctantly the actress let go Tristan's hand.

"Go on, director!" the pale Tristan urged. "Give us one true statement!"

"Terrible how, weeping innerly over lost love, I feel the glorious power of my freedom. Solitude is freedom and it does one in," the director said.

"I still don't understand," the actress said.

Tristan pounded his fist on the table, making the cups and plates leap up, and the actress flinched as if the unexpected blow had struck her in the face. "You stupid girl," he shouted, "can you still not see that we're talking about fidelity?"

"Yes, fidelity," the director said hollowly. "But let's leave the dining room and push on into Paris. It will do us good – perhaps."

3

The director, Tristan and the actress left the subway passages at Place Saint Michel. For her, everything about the Métro ride had been new and a part of Paris. For Tristan and the director it was tiresome routine. No successful city tour could result from the clash of a great curiosity and a twofold weariness. The actress had naturally imagined that the two men would show her Paris. Tristan, whom she had pestered with trifles on their subterranean journey, had remained mute. "How do people know what train to take?" she had asked, for example, and he pretended not to hear. "How often do the trains run?" she wanted to know a bit later and Tristan had grumbled, "They're simply there when they pull in." "Do the trains run all night?" she had wanted to know then and the director had rebuked her: "Now have done with your tourist's questions! They're an insult!" Through such questions and lack of answers the three fell into a bad mood. Once the director had decided "We're getting off here!" at the Saint Michel station, there was only silence between them. Silently they had walked through the stifling passages, and when they finally made it up the angular flights of stairs and into the open, an icy wind was blowing. Early November had arrived and it was nearly All Souls' Day.

"Hard to believe," the actress said into the oppressive silence, "that despite the blinding sun, it's one of the coldest days." But she received no answer because the countless pedestrians on Boulevard Saint Michel kept breaking up the little group, someone constantly rushing past between Tristan and the actress. Thus, vaguely hopeful, she took his arm.

Yet he was composed of a chill that seemed to press for distance, and she thought, "How difficult even the art of walking arm-in-arm is. Without drama school it would be unthinkable."

Since it was her first time in Paris, she would have liked to go shopping, but Tristan and the director left her no time for that. "What's the rush?" she asked the two men, whose renewed silence was like a rebuke. She only wanted confirmation that they really were in the Quartier Latin, but now she did not venture any further questions. She would find someone else. There were enough men on the streets of Paris. She did not need these two.

Tristan gave her a quick dry kiss on the lips. "You'll be disappointed, because we're so bitter, because we won't expound on beautiful Paris for you. Before your return journey, maybe you should book an official city tour. But we may say nothing about the city, nor can we permit you to window shop. You're here for a different reason." Then he fell silent again, and if it initially seemed he wanted only to catch his breath before going on, the actress soon realized the silence was not a pause but a cessation.

"Perhaps the actress is no actress at all, but only imagines her calling," the director thought at that moment. "But what else can she be?" he brooded, and the wind tousled everyone's hair.

"In winter the world is without reality." Tristan pointed his left hand at several bare trees near the Musée de Cluny. "It's an enormous silhouette and whoever wanted to tear the world to pieces now would have a particularly easy time of it."

"In winter the world is easier to manage," the director

suggested, "but any director worth his salt must also hold his own in rampant summer."

"Of course," Tristan nodded, his breath bursting in thick white puffs into the air.

They passed the book-filled windows of the Presses Universitaires and the director said, "Once I'd always have stopped in front of these windows. I would read the titles until one day it made me puke. My vomit streamed down the window panes. Of course I can't say whether I'd eaten too much before or whether the books disagreed with me. In any case I never stopped here after that."

The actress shuddered, briefly imagined the pastel-colored vomit running down the panes.

Not at all disgusted by it, Tristan picked up the story. "We all have our reasons that drive us from books," he said. "The only certainty is that, of all my friends who had spent decades reading, none reads anymore. One should look into this development." Then he raised his voice and, doubly loud, asked the actress, "So do you read books?"

"I love to read," she replied, astonished. But the director stamped his foot furiously on the pavement and shouted, "She won't warm up the day with that lukewarm manner."

Missing the sarcasm, she asked Tristan, "Now what have I done?"

Tristan shoved his hand into hers so they could stroll along swinging their arms like two high-spirited children. "You know," he told her, "our friend, the director, worries about the necessary fervor." He folded her small hand and laughed to himself.

They crossed Rue Soufflot. The Panthéon suddenly stood before them, but no one told the actress the building's name.

"When I was younger," Tristan said as they walked along the fence of the Luxembourg Gardens, "I came to these gardens almost daily. At the time I was touched by the sight of the playing children and their weary mothers." It did not amount to a conversation. Whatever was said fell like a single raindrop into a great barrenness and this barrenness was Tristan's sorrow, was the director's bitterness, was the actress's self-esteem.

"We're misunderstood, all three of us are misunderstood," the director droned and again the actress resisted him.

"How can you include me in your whining?" she asked. "I'm not the least misunderstood. On stage in Munich or Zurich or Vienna, I know I'm understood. The applause, each day wilder, proves it. It's just a question of expressing yourself clearly. You two of course are always secretive, and maybe that's your cover-up for not knowing what you want!" A gust of wind blew into her mouth and she fell silent, afraid of going hoarse. She was furious because her attack caused no reaction. Only Tristan shook his head almost imperceptibly, neither in affirmation nor in denial. It almost seemed the wind alone was making his head wobble. "Well, what do you say to that?" she asked once the wind had died down.

"Nothing." Tristan smiled. "But let me answer with a question that's preoccupied me for years: Why do you women always have to be so defensive? Why do you imagine we men constantly oppose you? Can't you see how tired and haggard most of us are even at birth? We aren't stronger than you and can't expect much from life. The few thinkers among us have always respected you and the animals pounce on you, on your outer shells, only because they're afraid of death. And why do you moan and cry out while making love, when we men usually remain quiet or only breathing hard? Because everything's more mysterious and beautiful for you? You can let yourselves go, occasionally at least. We always imagine we can't. Who are the truly oppressed?"

He had spoken the last phrases so somberly that the actress instinctively looked to the sky to see whether any light remained. She realized she would have to reply with particular care, for she was no longer speaking as an actress to Tristan, but as a woman for all women to a man for all men. She was about to mention male self-pity and rationalization when she remembered he was too intelligent for such a reply. But the rules of the game called for winning the day now, in conversation. "Give me time to respond," she said, "for I want to give you a valid answer."

Tristan made a bow as he walked.

But the director suddenly uttered the phrase on which all the troubles between men and women hang as if on a hook: "Rules of the game, nothing but stupid rules!" He gesticulated wildly. "Humanity's misery lies in its rules! Such wretched stammering about self-esteem, pride, duty toward the self! Everyone's absolute determination to take offence when offended! The insistence on retribution and revenge! How often do we feel nothing at all when something happens to us and yet we feel duty-bound to respond, to feel something when we don't really want to respond at all, when we don't really feel a thing? We're passive much of our lives and it's only the rules of the game that turn us against ourselves and others! On stage there are neither men nor women, but only parts played by men and women. And if we engage fully in the consummate arts, then male and female roles become interchangeable, because it's not the rules or the psychology that count any longer, but only the universal human surrender to death!" All at once the director no longer knew where he wanted his words to lead and he fell silent as quickly as the gusts of wind rose up and died down.

The three had reached Boulevard Montparnasse. They crossed the square and entered the Closerie des Lilas.

"Monsieur de la Cour," Tristan said to the pianist after they had spent a peaceful hour inside the restaurant, "would you please play Beethoven's *For Elise* for us?"

The pianist, a friend of Tristan's, smiled and made a mental note of the request. The actress, who had read on the wine list that she was sitting in the city's oldest literary café, cast theatrical glances at the other patrons, at the same time trying to conceal this from Tristan and the director. If she had not had the memory of passionate nights spent with Tristan in Munich, she would have suspected that the two men in front of her were misogynists, in love with each other. (Rules, always rules!)

And when the pianist began to play the request, Tristan said, more to himself than the others, "The only question is whether fidelity is also subject to the rules. That's the main question." He drank his campari soda with a straw, making little sucking noises, moving the straw deliberately along the fine line separating liquid and air.

"Always tending toward extremes," the director joked amiably. Again there was a minutes-long silence.

"My birthday's coming up," the director said, ignoring the piano, "and a few days before my birthday, I'm always seized by a panic to write something quickly, *before* the birthday's over. I want to deal with everything I consider important before the old year's past, to be cleansed and empty when the uncertainty begins."

"I understand you well," Tristan said, "for I was born in November too. At heart every man resembles the day and month of his birth. Thus I must remain somber all my life, and even if I do have occasional sunny periods or mild unthreatening ones, they're the exception. November has mild days too. When they occur we delight in their warmth, at the same time sensing that we're enjoying something forbidden."

"The only reason I moved to the hotel with you two was so I could finally sleep my fill," the director said, not picking up Tristan's thread. "I can sleep only in hotel beds. But even there I had an extraordinary experience last night: I awoke, having slept two or three hours and, groggy with sleep, I went to the window. Below me was the main intersection in front of the hotel, and I saw a large number of cars racing along like sadly guided toys. Then I went back to bed and slept two hours, only to go to the window again. I saw the same image and knew that these had to be different cars racing along like sadly guided toys. Everything below had changed, but the view and the sensations it gives rise to never change. I thought: It's a good lesson in relativity and immortality. Nothing ever changes, not even in the course of years, so long as we know how to see properly. Dying itself is nothing but a falling out of this invulnerable, senselessly functioning system that suffers no losses and passes death by. That's what I thought and suddenly found tears in my eyes. I slapped my own face hard and told myself: Now you've refuted your own directorial concept!"

The actress downed her fourth cognac. The director's speeches hardly concerned her anymore. But Tristan, who had strained to hear, grew reflective. "So that's how the night passed for you," he said softly, then cleared his throat and added somewhat more forcefully, "As for me, I watched the approaching dawn, thinking how sluggishly the night rises from such a long silence and great solitude."

"And yet solitude is an absolution," the director responded. "You, Tristan, have not yet understood the purity of solitude. You're too young. Of course we could hop into bed with the actress, make it a threesome. It might even be amusing. But I no longer want women. The last time I slept with a virgin was in Florence. There actually was an initial pain, there was actually blood at that penetration in the *European metropolis*. The girl was from the Calabrian backwoods, from the ends of the earth. I've long forgotten her face and name. It's always the origins I want to hang on to. But why am I talking of the present? What bad directorial habit is this? You must realize, Tristan, that it's all over for me. Here, with our actress, I'm directing for the last time. Look at her, the little lush. Her eyes have gone glassy, she's drunk and doesn't have the least idea she's part of a leave-taking."

"All at once you're a human being," Tristan said, "and no longer a spider." Never had the two been on such friendly terms.

The actress had slumped down. She had laid her head on her arms and fallen asleep. Tristan pointed at her and even the director took some pleasure in the sleeping woman. "She still owes us the answer she promised," he said.

"Don't be so cruel." Tristan smiled boyishly. "The answer owes itself."

4

He had expected it to be cold, and it was All Souls' Day. But even as he awoke late in the morning there was something cheerful about him. He whistled as he got up, something he never did otherwise, not even in spring. When he opened the window, warm air wafted into the room.

He had thought everyone would be at the cemeteries, but the streets were crowded with cars and pedestrians. The city lay open, only the graves were closed.

He was hungry and looking forward to a solitary breakfast in an old exclusive city café. But such eagerness was a sign of life that confused him, for he thought of it as a denial of All Souls' Day. Then again he had been prepared for the day of the dead. Perhaps the day was denying him and he was the one betrayed.

The sun shone brightly and warm, scattering his misgivings. How lovely death will have to be, he thought, if days commemorating the dead are so sweet.

He went out without his coat, intending to visit a cemetery, but he had no dead in this city. The discovery dismayed him and it was hard for him to get used to it. He entered the Caffè Greco and sat down in a corner facing Goethe's portrait and beside that of the child, Mario Gubinelli. The two subjects were dead, but their deaths had long become reconciled with life and so they lived again. They were not missed. He strove to think of some dead person he missed, but came up with no name. His commemorative mood seemed self-deceptive since, he had to admit, his dead provided him with a cushion. Those he loved he wished dead, so as not to lose them. He was pained only by voluntary separations from the living.

On the Piazza Mignanelli in the heart of Rome, he had his lunch served at an outside table, so warm was All Souls' Day. In front of him stood wine, oil and vinegar and a mixed salad in autumnal colors. Sometimes a wind stirred, making the edges of light and shadow flicker and dance. And from the wild vines overhanging the garden, leaves fell onto the plates of food, which delighted him. He stared at the green and yellow and red lettuce leaves. He was fascinated by the dark yellow oil and the cherry-red vinegar.

At the adjacent table sat two women, one kindly and old, the other young and spiteful. He looked at them until they looked back in confusion, and he silently appointed them his Roman dead. The day finally had to find its justification.

After his meal he hailed a cab and had himself driven to the Pyramid of Cestius, to the foreigners' cemetery. He walked among the rows of graves, but saw few visitors. Moss grew on Maria Obolensky's stony image, but someone had set a vase of flowers beside the monument. He was pleased by the gesture, but at the same time ashamed he had come empty-handed again. Wherever he went he received gifts, though he always came empty-handed himself. The cemetery was green and remote from November, unreal. "How repressed we northerners are!" he said. When he found himself standing beside Waiblinger's grave, he gave a nervous greeting and rushed off. Cats followed him. The animals seemed repugnant, they did not beg, but demanded and all were sick and marked for death. "Animals," he thought, and again and again: "Animals." Suddenly afraid of them, he ran from the quiet cemetery. Outside everything was as it had been.

In a narrow Roman lane boys and girls by the hundreds came toward him. School was out for the day. Yelling and running, the children pressed him against the wall. Cold now, he sadly missed his coat and only shrugged at the radiant sun. It was November, late autumn. All at once he felt sick and miserable, chattering with a sad joy. Tristan was himself again. And it was All Souls' Day throughout the world.

He proceeded to the Colosseum and sat down on a surviving stone bench. "Now I want to see my dead," he said to himself, "playing something cheerful for me on the proscenium below. Only on stage do the dead become tolerable human beings."

Later he indulged in the idea that on All Souls' Day all the cars in Roman traffic were driven by the dead, that is, by ghosts. For one day the living were dispensable.

On impulse he asked a young man who happened to be passing whether the day was a holiday. "Yes," the man answered, "the most important holiday, the day of the dead." Tristan nodded and thought, "Nowhere else would I have received this answer."

When he reached the Piazza di Spagna, the horse-drawn carriages were still tempting late tourists to make excursions. "*Signore, per piacere* ... ," a coachman offered. Tristan smiled, refusing. "This desperate attempt to prolong the season even to the point of denying death: how beautiful and painful." He did not say it aloud of course.

A man and boy passed by, the man's arm placed tenderly around the boy. Tristan watched the two, unaffected, although this gesture had once meant all the world to him.

"What's become of me in the meantime?" he asked himself sadly. "I'm afraid of beauty, and sexual lust plays tricks on me. It has me chase after certain people, then bids me grow cold and leave off, just when everything seems at hand and possible. I always exit alone."

As he walked on Tristan became sadder still. He was perplexed to find himself in Rome without being released by its spell. "Now not even Italy has a special landscape for me," he commiserated with himself. "Everywhere I go I carry my inner landscape along. So even travel has become pointless."

"Impossible to wake you." The director shook Tristan out of the Rome of his dreams. "Did you hear what I just said?"

"No, I didn't. What did you say?" Tristan replied indifferently.

"I said I want to write stage plays," the director repeated. "Apart from me, who else could create great tragedies these days?"

Tristan sat up in bed and tried to reduce Rome and the question to a common denominator. "The world of language," he said in a husky voice, "the world of language, no matter what it tries to describe or give form to, is totally sterile because, apart from the living, inanimate fact of the world, it contains its own reality it can never release. This knowledge of course is dreadful." A great yawn interrupted his last word. It had never been easy for Tristan to wake up.

"Listen," the director said. "Last night I wrote a poem I'd like your opinion on. Tell me what you think." He sat on the bed beside Tristan, cleared his throat and read. "I am olive wood/ and want to drift in water/ why is my world/

lacking the will of sponges/ to suck me full/ and fuller still/ till the olive wood I am/ can float no longer/ drunk on my own weight/ when I too am able/ to leave the surface/ leave behind the drifting/ swaying, being wooden/ and be at bottom/ a stone, no more a swimmer/ a bloodless ocean rock/ I swim, drift, am olive wood/ wooden I swim/ and am not wood/ my courage is deep/ untroubled my sleep." He cleared his throat again. "What do you think?"

Tristan was wide-awake now. "In a writer's life," he said quickly, "there's the near certainty that his function is *childish*, that he's cheating time itself, that it's ridiculous to keep opposing the powers of the vulgar, the tangible, with mind and word games. The writer resists this terrible realization only with his incurable *child-likeness*. Sorry for not speaking clearly, but I've just been somewhere else entirely." He climbed out of bed and went to the bathroom.

"But it's terribly late!" he called through the closed door. "We must hurry to the actress at once!" As he quickly dressed, he was seized by doubt and a guilty conscience. Though he had made no precise date with the actress, he suddenly felt guilty. And she would surely have preferred Tristan to spend the nights in her room. After all the two had sworn their undying love years ago, and part of this rash promise had surely survived, or why else had he summoned her to Paris? Small wonder that she had felt like the victim of a practical joke from the time she arrived. Tristan almost felt sorry for the duped actress. He almost wanted to run to her, take her tenderly in his arms and apologize for his behavior. But he could not afford to indulge in such weakness, not yet, since the alchemy of exaltation had hardly begun to take effect on her.

Tristan noticed how deeply he had become mixed up in the director's coordinates. At first he had wanted nothing from the actress but a chance to revive an old passion, since new passions no longer existed for him. He had attached no metaphysical goals or expectations to the invitation. At bottom he had wanted only what he now denied himself and her: a little tenderness, a few nights of pleasure, a past become present – denied, because he did sense a kind of passion flare up within him, that of obedience to the director. The poor actress! She had, Tristan thought fleetingly, unwittingly run into the trap of two lunatics. He wondered why, since her arrival, he had felt strictly bound to the director who had meant nothing to him before. Only a few days ago Tristan had thought of him as a frustrated Parisian guide and had smiled indulgently at his constant references to direction: A likable fool, there are so many . . . But now he loved the director and would not think of criticizing him. He considered him an authority. Without him, no blood would flow through his veins. And if Tristan really were to sleep with the actress, he would have to find a way to include the director in their lovemaking.

When Tristan was dressed he accompanied the director to the actress's room, where he tried the door handle without knocking first. It was open and the two men entered.

The actress was sitting at the window. She was reading a paper and did not seem to notice her two visitors come in. She read and occasionally looked out the window. The blankets and sheets of her bed lay in disarray. Tristan still felt the desire to speak intimately with her, but it seemed to him that the director, who said nothing, would dictate a harsher language.

"You're already up and dressed," Tristan said sternly, "because you slept in the café yesterday." He stood behind the chair on which she was sitting.

"You're wrong," she replied, pretending to read her paper, "and in case you're interested, I went out again last night. It was already late and you two were sleeping. I didn't return to the hotel till morning, and I wasn't alone, but I don't feel tired because I had a lovely night." Her voice sounded clear and indifferent. The actress knew her revelation would shock Tristan, which was just what she wanted.

He immediately positioned himself in front of the seated woman and looked at her in dismay. "You went out?" he said. "Why didn't you tell us what you had in mind? We would of course have shown you Paris by night!"

"Precisely," she laughed. "The *two* of you would have, but *one* escort's enough for me and he was easy enough to find."

Bewildered Tristan looked to the director, who had sat down in an easy chair. The director smiled. He had turned into a spider once again.

"You did it to hurt me!" Tristan struck the paper from the actress's hands. "You've been in Paris only three days," he raged, "and already you're reading German newspapers!"

She reacted calmly to his fit of rage. "Yes, I read German papers," she said, "and beyond that I look out the window. It's lovely to see the blackbirds perched on the branches, and when I consider how naked the world's become once more, then I never want to see naked people again. Let them be clothed and doubly clothed to compensate for nature. One hour at this window is enough to snuff out all sensuality."

"And surely you, who want to see people clothed, slept with a man last night!" Tristan said.

The actress stood up. "Yes I did and it was lovely."

Tristan trembled and staggered toward the window. "How can you hurt me in this way?"

"I can hurt you in any way whatsoever," she answered very calmly. "But I haven't hurt you. I merely experienced the most natural thing in the world and I owe nothing to Tristan or any other man."

He hoped the director would come to his aid by raising an objection. But the director remained silent, a smiling spider.

"You've totally changed overnight," Tristan remarked flatly and sat down in the chair on which the actress had just been sitting. The wood was still warm from her body, but he thought he could discern her previous night's passions in this warmth. The paper lay on the floor like an enormous desiccated butterfly. "Why have you changed so much?"

"I haven't changed," she said. "Now I'm only the actress. I'm always the way I am now. Only when I arrived in this city to see you was I different, and yesterday too. I wanted to come to my Tristan as a woman, not as the actress. I wanted again to be that woman with whom Tristan slept in Munich. It was an experiment and a hope, but Tristan was no longer the timid, shyly seductive boy I met in Munich years ago. I gave the metamorphosed man plenty of time to recall the potential for a miracle. But yesterday in the Closerie des Lilas, I fell asleep waiting. Then I came to my senses again," she said, "and the past night was the present, nothing more."

"Then this night must be the past for you now," Tristan replied in dismay.

"Past, just as Tristan is," she confirmed.

He rested his chin on his hands. "And all my life I was fool enough to think that no one but me was gathering up the past," he said under his breath. He sighed. "I'd imagined that I and I alone was capable of fidelity. Now I must assume another fidelity also exists."

The actress laughed wantonly, as though a child were amusing her with merry games. She approached and kissed him. He accepted the kiss with parted lips, but could summon no strength to respond. The kiss found a man without any will. "You're such a dear, Tristan," she laughed, "but tell me, are my caresses inferior now that I've slept with a chance acquaintance?"

Tristan, who had wanted to bring about the actress's exaltation, suddenly saw himself as a schoolboy. The director kept silent, but stared into his eyes.

The actress was refreshingly beautiful.

5

"When we like someone," the director said, "we belittle him with our affection. We push him closer to our own standards and when's he's reached them, we love him. We aggrandize people who mean nothing to us until they become repulsive to us. Two people who love each other have brought each other to the denominator that suits them. Now if such people separate, only to meet again some time later, then they're shocked by each other: their absence has allowed them to regain their natural proportions. Now the process of belittlement should be resumed, but it rarely succeeds a second time. Thus indifference and hatred may well turn to love, but between one love and another few bridges are built. So much for your new encounter." He lit a cigarette without asking Tristan and the actress whether they also cared to smoke.

"I'm of the opinion that we should take the actress out among human beings," Tristan said. "If we always keep to ourselves we'll only hurt one another. Certainly you, director, are used to solitude, nor does it bother me, but the actress seems to need other company. Let's introduce her to our little circle – your circle, actually. In any case, I've always considered myself a marginal figure."

"A marginal figure defines a group's limits without necessarily adding to it in any way," the director replied. "I'd rather have kept the actress out of the circle of my guests, but if Tristan wants to arrange a meeting, I'll inform them." He pulled a leather-bound address book from his coat pocket and began to dial a number. He spent fifteen minutes on this task while Tristan and the actress looked at each other in stalwart silence. "We'll meet tonight in the usual place," the director then announced.

"It sounds like a conspiracy," the actress laughed, but he sternly demanded, "Don't laugh, actress!" The ritual of breakfast was repeated, without sunlight this time. Tristan insisted on a different table near the kitchen entrance.

"But that's the worst spot," the actress protested. "Why should we put up with the draft from the swinging door, the annoying kitchen smells and the commotion of sweaty waiters?"

"That's just what I love," Tristan said. "This totally useless, yet indispensable bustle reassures me for another brief hour that life is absurd and wonderful."

"And your guest's wishes count for nothing." She sulked as they sat down at the table designated by Tristan.

"I haven't yet told you that I was in Rome today," he said to change the subject. "It was mild and sunny on the day I spent there, and I was in all the places where Rome becomes *my* city. I was surprised how few people were at the cemetery: today is All Souls' Day. But who knows, perhaps the new cemeteries are more crowded. As for me, I was at my cemetery of the illustrious forgotten again. Rome. Yes, I have a special affinity with Rome. I never yearn for the city, but I always feel at home there as soon as I arrive. I love Rome with the same composure with which one should love a woman."

"But you only dreamed you were in Rome," the actress said.

"Your objection carries no weight," Tristan said.

And so they concluded even this breakfast, which the

director had hardly touched this time. "Now let's finally go into town," he said, yawning. He wore a drab tie that perfectly matched his yawning.

Tristan, who usually paid no attention to clothing, noticed the hopeless color. He pointed a finger at the director. "Even though the director had no idea when getting dressed that he would be meeting his guests today, he still put on his drab tie. You should know, dear actress, that with this tie he hopes to avoid people's looks."

"The better for me to hold sway over them," the director said.

The actress said nothing. They set off.

The two men's thoughts and observations increasingly bored and frightened her. She thought about the lover she had picked up last night and wished she were back in his magical arms. She entertained the idea of packing her bags, leaving the hotel and the two madmen and spending what little time she had left in Paris on her own. Then Tristan asked the director, "Will Sebastian, the mime, also be coming today?"

The actress pricked up her ears. A man called Sebastian had been her lover the previous night. His sensitive fingers had given her an unworldly pleasure. She would not be able to forget the man. But Sebastian had refused to entrust her with his address. He had shaken off her curiosity with a laugh and said, "Once is enough, you ravishing actress!" Now at the mention of Sebastian, the mime, she was almost convinced it was her Sebastian. She ached to be back in his arms, and if Tristan or the director could unwittingly make another encounter possible, she was prepared to spend the rest of the day with the two men who had become insufferable, so long as the evening restored the mime to her. "What are you saying?" she asked, not waiting for the director to answer. "You know a mime called Sebastian? What does he look like?"

But the director dashed her impassioned question. "Silence, actress! Our friends are no concern of yours!" But to Tristan he calmly said, "Yes, Sebastian will also be coming to convince us of the futility of words."

She smiled at that. Though her smile originated in the senses, she resembled a Madonna carved of wood.

But Tristan, startled by her curiosity, had become keen of hearing. "Do you happen to know the mime?" he asked with an insidious sweetness. She did not answer and the director looked to the sky, checking the state of the weather. Tristan suddenly knew he would never be able to exalt the actress.

"The mime is no ascetic, but a sensual man who knows how to express himself sensually. This by way of definition," the director said.

"Yes," the actress sighed, momentarily all *woman*.

"No," Tristan said. "No!"

"What are you denying?" The director stopped in his tracks.

"I don't know why I said no," Tristan remarked casually and likewise stopped.

The actress meanwhile had walked on. From a distance she reproached them. "If all you can do is stop and talk then of course we'll never get into Paris!"

The director and Tristan flinched as if roused from a light slumber. They rushed to the indignantly waiting actress, and as they hurried along, they began to drag their feet.

"You're walking like old men," she said.

A cab came up the street. Tristan signaled the driver, who pulled over in front of them. Tristan and the actress sat in the back, the director beside the driver. The director gave their destination and during the half-hour ride not another word was said.

Tristan stared at the still seductively soft skin of the actress's face. She gazed out the window. He desired her, above all he wanted her skin. He wanted to nestle in this lovely skin, kiss, claw, force his way in. His eyes roamed greedily over her throat. He tried again to imagine the nakedness of this woman he had once had and enjoyed for many a night. But the image that materialized remained blurred and interchangeable. "This lack of sharp definition lends itself poorly to an exaltation," he thought.

The cabdriver jolted along recklessly. The flowing images of the city were distorted and fragmented. When they had reached their destination, three exhausted people got out of the cab.

The actress breathed in the air, deeply and audibly. The director said, "Don't breathe so shamelessly, you voracious actress! Actors always want to use up all the world's air. But it's just you actors who need the least air, since the stage is part of the universe, the cosmos."

Tristan felt another crisis coming on. The actress did not understand. She wanted to give a response, was about to fly into a rage, when he spread his arms wide like a bird. At that she held her tongue and gaped in awe at Tristan, whose movements had conjured up her silence.

"Dear actress," he said, "let's not make the day hard for

each other. I have the feeling this is our last day. As we walk through this lovely Paris, I will by your leave tell you something about fidelity. Tonight you will meet our circle, and the people we'll introduce you to do not absolutely believe in fidelity. Rather they believe in infidelity. But infidelity need not be given expression, it expresses itself. Only fidelity, actress, requires thought – and words perhaps. Hear me out on fidelity. It shouldn't detract from your stroll through Paris and you can window shop as you listen. I don't want to interfere, actress. I just want to take advantage of this final opportunity."

"Don't keep calling me *actress*," the actress flared up, "for basically I'm no actress at all. I *was* an actress, but now I'm heading in other directions."

"No sooner do you speak of fidelity," the director said, "than some actress becomes unfaithful! Now she even denies her calling. She says she's no longer an actress only to be unfaithful and to give the lie to your good intentions, Tristan."

"No, that's not why I've finally divulged my secret," she said. "I'm just fed up with your label, which no longer fits. I hate the two of you. You're impossible!" Her voice cracked on the last words.

"Don't get excited, please," Tristan said. "Naturally we're surprised when you suddenly deny your calling. You've never disputed it before, so it necessarily confuses us. Explain yourself, dear presumptive actress."

His gentle words humanized her. She stared at each of them in turn. She too had stopped on the sidewalk, not infrequently presenting an obstacle to passers-by, without realizing it of course. "If you two laughable refugees lived in

Germany," she said haughtily, "you'd also know I only spend half the season on our stages. Everyone knows where I spend the rest of the year. But you two, who pretend to be my confidants, don't know." Her voice was a mix of contempt and pride and coldness.

"No, we don't," Tristan said, and the director added, "But we want to know. Explain yourself here and now, presumptive actress! We fugitives demand an explanation!"

"Very well," she said. "Over the years I've come to realize that stage-acting has brought me less and less satisfaction. Close friends and important critics have often pointed out that I have not only a speaking voice that carries well, but also a singing voice that could be developed. For some years I've felt more and more irresistibly drawn to music. I can no longer deny the world my singing voice, my real talent. Music means more to me than speech. In the near future I'll be giving up the theater for the opera. I hardly think of myself as an actress anymore. For seven months of the year I live high in the mountains near Como. There I work on my singing voice – and believe me it's coming along, yes it's coming! Twice a week I take the train to Milan. There I study dramatic singing with the world-renowned Cavalcanti."

"She studies singing with Cavalcanti," the director shrieked, beside himself. "She dares turn her back on the sacred stage! She lets herself be duped by a fat whore of a singer! She betrays the German stage with Cavalcanti!" His words came spilling out. "I ought to strangle you on the spot for your infidelity to the stage. You're no actress, quite right. You are nothing, you've annulled yourself. An actor can only destroy himself, but never can he become somebody else."

The actress laughed hysterically, but Tristan laid his hands on the shaking director's shoulders. "Don't be angry with her, friend," Tristan appeased him as he raged. "What does a woman, singer or actress know about fidelity? And Cavalcanti can't understand very much about voices or she'd know that our voices are written in the stars. But these we cannot alter. Only now, good director, do I realize how much the dear misguided actress deserves our pity. Don't be angry with her but feel sorry for her."

The director was still shaking. "Speak of fidelity," he urged Tristan. "Speak forthwith of fidelity, even if it's already far too late."

6

"Since a person can feel difficulty, pain or grief grow inside and seem to become insurmountable, and since a person can grow along with his difficulties, I will tell you about fidelity," Tristan said to the actress. "Of course the difficulty, pain or grief can overwhelm the person and destroy him, so that at one blow he feels inconsequential, though in truth he's become a victim, stifled, deserving our pity. Oh my dear presumptive actress, do you know the sorrow the sorrowful man imparts to and sees in everything around him? The happiness the happy man sees everywhere? For all that the phenomena around us are only like dead matter. Even the famous Parisian moonlight, even sunsets are nothing. How this realization saddens one."

"I'm not saying a thing," the actress said.

They walked on to Place de la Madelaine. All at once it grew very noisy around them. A crowd of people thickened into a large mass, swelled up and suddenly vanished again: German tourists, belated travelers who had wound their insecurities into a large communal ball in which Paris nearly became entangled.

"Like anything that threatens me," the director said, "I love even these aliens. They don't recognize me and that's just as well. I experience my race only as a horde vacationing abroad. Never do I let on that I'm one of them, and so I experience their ill-bred consternation and their often exquisite difficulties. I only hear snatches of German and, occasionally, distorted voices on the radio. It's not much. Nevertheless, these people and their voices all sound enchanted abroad, happier than at home. To avoid being pitied as an exile by those I ought to pity for their domiciles, I never reveal myself, as I've already said. But every encounter, always a sickly whirlwind – you've just witnessed that turbulence – moves me almost to tears. For seconds I imagine that these creatures understand my language. But then I get over it and spend hours reproaching myself for my thoughts. This too, I presume, touches on the terrible question of fidelity."

"What lovely crystal glasses!" The actress suddenly stopped in front of a large glittering display. "I'm crazy about this crystal," she said. "I'm going in to buy these elegant glasses! Wait here for me, you two." And she had already vanished inside the shop.

"Her world is all make-up and disorder," Tristan said to the director, "and yet the actress wants to convince us that we're sick and in the wrong. Because we're far too sensitive for these stifling streets, we can't even refute her articulately. We're too restrained, we're not breathing properly and our amateurish technique puts us in the wrong. Right and wrong, director, aren't values in themselves. They cling lifelessly to the art of recitation. Proper breathing – the actress has surely learned that from Cavalcanti. But where did we learn how to breathe?"

"Here we are waiting for the actress. When she comes out of the shop she'll ask one of us to carry her parcel," the director said to himself in a monotone. "Will we carry her parcel? Of course we will. Will we keep trying to speak of fidelity? Yes, we'll try. You especially, Tristan, must reveal your past. Speak of the black sails, don't be ashamed of them, good friend. Will the actress listen to your words? No, she won't. But no matter. The alchemy of exaltation works despite resistance, it can penetrate crystal, it will penetrate the actress. Above all, Tristan, speak of the black sails."

"I'm not much good at walks," Tristan said. "Out on the street I see more clearly and recognize that all the lovely young women are stealing along bent over slightly, only faking their upright gait. In fact they're hags, and the eyes of many a youth and man expose a compulsive murderer. I suffer from walking along in a hyper state, taking in so many impressions that, finally exhausted, I can hardly manage another step."

The actress, loaded down and with an idiotic smile on her face, came out of the shop. Her face had assumed the bold lines of modern wine glasses and she was brimming over with her winsome, burdensome artificiality. "I've always wanted glasses like these," she said, and not until she looked at Tristan and the director, stiffly and indifferently watching her entrance, did she recall their frame of mind. She stopped smiling, her lips narrowed and tensed, the scene was reestablished.

"Which one of you will carry my parcel?" she asked without cajoling.

"No one," Tristan answered indifferently. "Instead we'll call a cab and have the driver take it back to the hotel." With these words he hailed a passing cab and explained the situation to the driver. The actress wanted to protest, but Tristan had already taken the parcel from her hands and stowed it in the back seat. The cab drove off.

"What guarantee do I have," she said, "that this man really will deliver my parcel?"

Tristan smiled, a touch of malice on his features. Very

loudly, the director said, "You have no guarantee of the parcel's safe arrival. Nor is one needed. Only Germans keep insisting on such ridiculous assurances. The parcel will arrive, though there's no guarantee."

Agitated, the actress said, "Then at least we should have taken down the license number."

"What for?" Tristan said, still smiling. "Why must you Germans, who betray every confidence, always mistrust the world's innocent creatures and things? I love how you all squirm with anxiety."

"Prejudices! You two are capable of nothing but prejudices!" She twisted her face into an ugly grimace. The director seized her firmly by the wrist. She cried out in pain and tried unsuccessfully to escape his violent grip. Passersby gaped at the scene in surprise, but all hurried on to avoid becoming involved. But the actress turned and almost dropped to her knees, so much pain was the director causing her.

Tristan stood by unconcerned, not trying to help her in word or deed.

"I'll scream for help," she threatened. "I'll cry rape!" She was close to tears.

But the director was enjoying her unladylike contortions. "Stay as you are," he warned the struggling woman. "Don't make any sudden moves, you treacherous presumptive actress, or you'll drop from the strings that guide you along." So saying he released her from his rough grasp.

Staggering, she brushed the hair from her brow with one hand and stared at him with expressionless, dimly blazing eyes. Her breath was labored.

"What breathing – as if you'd just made love," the

director raved, already a thousand years removed from what had happened.

But Tristan became businesslike. "Why do you speak of the actress in terms of a *puppet*?" he asked him.

The actress pressed against the store wall, crouched and stretched. Tristan and the director, preoccupied with each other and themselves, ignored her.

"Of course we're puppets, Tristan," the director said. "Even our names – we don't so much bear them as we are tied to them. Everyone calls me the director. I call myself the director. I've long forgotten my first and last names that foundered under the weight of my direction. Or take the actress – she too is nameless. We have such disdain for her wish to become a singer only because her title will no longer fit once she starts singing. Yet we can't give her any other name. Already we're treading on thin ice: we call the actress *actress* to be sure, but each time we do we think the name is fundamentally wrong. We say the word and in doing so, seek a firm hold, but at the same time give ourselves a jolt that will upset us soon enough. Indeed it seems as if my name and hers were not real ones, but job designations, as if you alone bore a genuine name. But this impression is deceptive. For your sorrow is your job and I expect mastery in all occupations. We are puppets. The nylon strings of direction, acting and sorrow push and pull us through the world, through Paris, and for all that our gallant movements remain stiff and lifeless. Onlookers laugh at us, serious people turn their backs. Our own inclinations pull the strings, our emotions guide us. But we're bad puppets because we're not lifeless. Just look at the actress, how she trembles and breathes, how alive she is, this treacherous actress . . ."

Tristan, who had been watching the director intently, now turned to her. She was still leaning against the building's brownstone wall. Beside her, glass and crystal sparkled in the large display window. She had adopted an animal-like stance. Crouched tightly against the wall, she seemed no living being, but part of the wall, like a fossil chiseled free or a grotesque sculpture. He regarded the metamorphosed actress for a long time, freezing and shivering as he did so. "You poor thing," he said to her. "How you've changed since our nights in Munich." He wanted to go to her and stroke her hair, but she let out a cry, pushed herself from the wall and ran off. Tristan and the director watched her, spellbound, so energetic had her movements suddenly become.

"But because she's held by strings, she only appears to be running. In truth her charming, lifeless feet aren't even touching the ground," the director suggested sadly.

"Where could she be running now?" Tristan asked, himself more than the director, who replied, "Back to us of course. The stage is quite small and the strings are short."

The two began to miss the actress as soon as she had disappeared around the first corner.

"For all our rancor, how we depend on her," Tristan sighed, but the director laughed. They waited irresolutely. Nothing but the crystal seemed certain.

Tristan said, "I love the actress, but don't know how to show it. And I can well imagine that our attempt at exaltation will fail. Then we'll stay in exile even more obstinately. I'd dearly like to speak to her of fidelity, but she's run off."

"And will go around the block and return," the director said.

"When we have her back," Tristan said, "we'll take her to the Jardin des Plantes. Rilke wrote some of his best poems there. But we won't tell her that. Instead we'll take her to the serpentarium. Maybe she has an aversion to snakes. I love them, as you surely do, director. In front of the snake terraria, we'll speak to her of fidelity."

The actress appeared as if aged and with her hair disheveled. She made an effort to look natural and to play down her flight.

"Why did you come back?" Tristan asked the breathless woman.

She tried to laugh, but her lungs were greedily sucking in air and the laughter sounded like rattling. "Why?" she said. "Why? Why? I'll tell you why I've come back. But first let me tell you why I ran off. You disgusted me. I couldn't stand the sight of you any longer. But no sooner had I reached a different street – no Tristan, no director – than I remembered just how sleazy and ridiculous you were. I stopped running, I sauntered around the block and now I'm back. From now on the two of you won't be able to rile me. Running away from you would mean taking you seriously, and so here I am."

"We missed you, presumptive actress, and now we have you back. You don't take us seriously, but despite that, you've remained faithful to us. I think that's splendid," Tristan said.

"It seems more important to be faithful than to take a person seriously and so punish him by being unfaithful," the director philosophized.

"You're singing the same old song," the actress said.

"Yes, you're right," Tristan said. "We're true to ourselves and you have remained true to us. Perhaps fidelity is a question of not taking things seriously."

"You should comb your hair and straighten your jacket and blouse," the director told the actress. "After all, we don't want to go to the Jardin des Plantes with a tramp. We owe this beautiful Paris a modicum of external order."

She readily complied. Meanwhile Tristan and the director took a step back. She brushed her reddish hair and parted it with a golden pocket comb. It was a cold and gusty November day. The scene contained an element of the Versailles kings' *lever*.

"We're exposing our secret royalty to the commoners," Tristan whispered to the director.

But he coughed scornfully. "I am so stuffed with blue blood I'm like an inkwell. I write my scripts to rid myself of my aristocracy. But still my veins suffer from high pressure and if I don't explode first, my blue blood will flood and drown the world. What, pale Tristan, do you or the silly actress know about such agonies? I envy the two of you and yet pity you for your anemic weakness!"

The actress meanwhile had finished and turned away from the display window. Calm and defiant, she looked the two men in the eyes. "It's noon already," she said, "and tonight we're going to meet the mime. It will no doubt be a mute, but eloquent evening." There was no sign of her recent outburst.

"Quick as women are to regain their composure, they're as quick to recover their appetite for everything," the director declared in a professorial tone.

The actress ignored him. "Where to now?"

"We're going to the Jardin des Plantes," Tristan answered. "It's a beautiful garden with beautiful halls and a beautiful museum. We could have taken you to the Louvre, but we don't want to burden you, presumptive actress, with the standard experience of an utterly immaculate collection. Let the tours crowd into the Louvre while we go to the Jardin des Plantes. Nowhere else in Paris, with the possible exception of the splendid morgue, can we better learn about ephemerality than where we're taking you."

Her suspicions had become aroused. "Jardin des Plantes, morgue, ephemerality?" she said syllable by syllable. "You must tell me what it's all about."

But the director said, "Come on, let's get going! Things will explain themselves."

Tristan took her arm and pulled her along.

"But tonight we're meeting the mime," she said. "We are meeting the mime tonight, aren't we?" Not until he had clearly assured her that they would indeed be meeting him did she allow herself to be led more willingly and she fell into rhythmical step with her escorts. Through the city's confined and open spaces they finally reached the large iron fence and gates outside the Jardin des Plantes. "Nature doesn't mean much to me," she announced.

"And you don't mean much to nature," the director said. "One little bite," he added softly, "and neither theater nor opera would be betrayed by a foolish woman."

They crossed a busy intersection. "What does he mean by that?" the actress asked Tristan, who had not spoken the whole way because their rhythmical gait had drawn him into a wondrous spell, had ensnared and entangled him.

"Enjoy the dead flowers, presumptive actress," he finally muttered when they had passed beneath the black and gold latticed arch and were beset by man-sized leafless rose bushes.

7

"All my life I've enjoyed dealing with snakes," Tristan told the actress and the director when they entered the serpentarium. Musty, humid air wafted against them, but she alone started back. Tristan and the director kept their composure even now.

"It's unbearable here. Where are we exactly?" Her voice sounded hostile.

"In the heart of Paris," Tristan announced somewhat ostentatiously and somewhat mysteriously. "We're in the land of wonderful deaths. Here it's a question of being true to life, and I'll tell you why I love snakes." He cleared his throat as if preparing for a formal speech. But the actress thought she was being made a fool of, insulted again. Nor did she see any snakes in the large glass-roofed area, since the crocodiles were housed in this first hall, one of Europe's largest crocodile collections of which the zoo could well be proud. The sluggish reptiles barely moved. Many of them lay hidden in the slimy water, only their walleyes and bubble-spewing nostrils jutting out. The basins were sunk several yards into the ground, so that visitors found themselves looking down through dark green bars at animals that stirred more nausea than fear.

"I don't see any snakes," the actress said, "and I think taking me to the zoo shows very poor taste. I have better ways to pass the time in Paris."

Tristan stepped up close to her. It appeared as if they were on stage and he about to entrust her with a secret. "The crocodiles are only the prelude, dear presumptive actress," he whispered. "We can reach the small manners of death only via the detour of great horrors, as everyone knows. And as for your criticism of our coming here, let me kindly remind you that you didn't come to Paris to pass the time."

The director seemed to be giving the sleepy reptiles his undivided attention. He leaned so far over the railing that he was in danger of toppling into the basin.

The actress stared silently at him for some seconds before calling to Tristan, "Yes, I know, you want to pester me again with your notion of exaltation. I want to hear no more about it. Your madness is making my ears ache."

"But not a trace of heartache," the director said, suddenly alert, obviously having not only gazed at every crocodile scale but also listened to every syllable.

"No, not a trace of heartache!" Her words were distorted and echoed by the ceiling and walls so that only a ragged smacking sound hung in the air. But Tristan would not be distracted. He went straight across the hall to the door that led to the snakes. The director and actress followed as if he were the natural leader.

Thus they came into the second hall, which lacked the crocodile hall's lofty bright ceiling. Pale neon tubes cooled and inadequately lit the low room. Along the walls were a few dozen medium-sized windows behind which multicolored lights were glowing, some only faintly.

"Like stages for a puppet-show!" the actress said and the director scoffed nasally, "Are you all being good, boys and girls?"

But for the three of them, there were no visitors in the elongated room. "Whether we're all being good, that is the question," Tristan said very softly, as if addressing no one, but then he grew louder. "So long as the glass panes are locked our visit remains a happy image. Yet if they're opened, reality itself will open to us."

Bored, the actress laughed. "Are you trying to scare us with your half-dead snakes?" Defiantly, she added, "I know you two are childish, but I'm no longer a child."

Tristan placed his right index finger over his mouth, then reached for her with one hand, for the director with the other and so pulled the two up to the first of the displays. "Take a good look at the lock." He pointed at the simple mechanism that held the panes in place. "It's a German patent," he explained. "Every display in this room is locked according to the same principle. Two panes on guide rails: the right can be pushed to the left, the left to the right. Like a glass case for knickknacks. But now to the lock – a thin metal strip, notched on both sides and hooked on one end, is inserted between the two panes, right in the middle of the display case. Look here." He pointed out the curvature of the adjustable metal strip that fit perfectly around the polished end of one pane. In the middle of the case the two panes overlapped about an inch. But for the length of a middle finger the notched metal strip lay across the inner pane. "Now for the truly marvelous thing about this simple lock!" Tristan pointed to a small chrome cylinder through the back of which the metal strip ran. Its face revealed a keyhole. He demonstrated by rattling the cylinder, which sat firmly on the metal strip and would not budge. "Great, isn't it?" he said. "Only the cylinder holds the strip in place and it alone keeps the panes from being shifted open. All one needs is the right key and the tiny safeguard would slide from the metal strip, from the pane, from human beings!" He stopped, taking quick breaths.

"Why so idiotically worked up?" the actress asked. "I've seen thousands of these gadgets. Not an hour ago at the crystal shop I saw the same unwieldy things. They were used to secure particularly valuable glass items. Poor Tristan, I'm almost convinced you need special care." She spoke earnestly, without irony.

But Tristan, who had caught his breath again, ignored her. "Two little metal objects," he said, "lying on the terrarium floor, loose and without apparent connection when separated. But joined, they're a part of the prison that keeps us from the snakes and the snakes from us."

The director bent down to the small white sign that briefly described the species and habits of snakes to be marvelled at here. "And just what do we have here?" he said to himself and, calmly ignoring Tristan's agitation, read out the information. "The Australian Death Adder, the Australian Death Adder, well well."

Tristan was still enthusing over the cylindrical lock. "Whoever has the key that, incidentally, fits all the locks, has access to these manners of death!"

The actress grimaced and yawned demonstratively. "But who has this key?"

Tristan was still caught up in his lecture. "But I ask you, who has this key? Why the snake-keeper of course, the snake-keeper has a key. When the serpentarium is closed to the public, he must clean the terraria, feed the animals: live mice, live rats. A snake never eats anything dead. It would rather starve ... The snake-keeper has a key. His work is no joy, though it may well be a passion ... And the snake-keeper – "His voice was cracking – " ... the snake-keeper is responsible for locking up the displays. The snake-keeper is responsible for the snakes!" His face, which had just been aglow with excitement, assumed its usual pallor again and the customary sorrow returned to his features. Tristan had been reduced to Tristan again as he wearily said, "The snake-keeper loves his snakes. He knows them, he feeds them year after year. He helps them shed their skins. He wants them to have young, which they never do in captivity. He knows how easily the slightest draft can prove fatal for a snake: within a few hours it's dead. But no snake knows its keeper." He paused a moment, then continued. "The snake-keeper can expect no friendship. Even after years the animals don't recognize him. They're all nearly blind, they don't see him, they only sense the movements of his warm hand at which they lunge – eager for prey or out of fear. They hardly think and do not feel. They are merely beautiful. They're never cold and slimy, but warm and soothing – like human skin. One can't help but love them, though snakes never reciprocate this love." As he talked, he had become increasingly quiet. Now he was silent. He stared through the glass into the terrarium and only the trio's breathing could be heard.

"In four hours we're going to meet the mime," the actress said abruptly. "I'll ask him to mimic a snake. That will impress me more than your incoherent babble, Tristan." Her voice filled the room with ice.

But Tristan who had just been lost in thought, was suddenly alert. "The actress, who's no longer an actress and who otherwise is nothing," he roared at the director, "has no use for intimacies, for metaphors, for subtle shadings. We won't be able to spare her from reality. Who did I say has the key to the small locks? Did I say the snake-keeper has the key? Did I say that? And did I say who the snake-keeper is? Who the snake-keeper was?"

All at once the actress was afraid of Tristan, whom she had never seen so worked up. The director left them, went to the only door and stood straddle-legged in front of it, as if standing guard. Tristan suddenly held a heavy bunch of keys in his hand, dozens of them in all shapes and sizes. He seemed to be looking for one in particular. Fearful and spellbound, the actress stared at him. He took a small key between his thumb and index finger and held it up. His whole body stretched and seemed to grow as, high above, the little key sparkled like an ill-boding star.

"What are you doing?" she asked softly, but her question did not sound like one.

With a bounce in his step, Tristan went to the display case, lowered the still raised hand that held the little key, which he inserted into the cylinder's slot, turned 180 degrees and already the cylinder could be slipped off the metal strip. The panes could be opened.

The actress cried out. Like most people, she hated and feared snakes. She screamed out of mortal fear and loathing, saw the adder crawl up her skin, felt its deadly bite, though she had no idea what the snake looked like nor the manner of its bite. She ran screaming to the exit, where the director blocked her path, ran back into the hall's center, breathlessly stared at Tristan, screamed and felt the convulsive horror of death, though he had not opened the panes even a finger's breadth. She collapsed and began to weep. "Why are you toying with me like this?" she sobbed. "What have I done to you?"

At that Tristan and the director approached the woman cowering on the floor, gripped her by the arms and pulled her to her feet, wiped the hair from her tear-soaked face and said, each for himself and yet in chorus, "You poor, dear presumptive actress. We're so fond of you." And Tristan kissed her brow, the director her hands. She looked around, eyes wide and swollen, saw not snakes, but only two men and it seemed to her as if she had just come out of a fainting spell.

Tristan's eyes were brimming with tears. He was weeping.

The director stepped back a few paces. He seemed very tired.

"Why are you crying, Tristan?" The actress wiped a tear from his cheek. She had unexpectedly become the consoler.

This bewildered him and even disconcerted the director, who blinked as though blinded by an unexpected light. "Maybe she's an actress after all and her infidelity can be attributed to her talent," he thought.

Tristan was enjoying the tender gesture just bestowed on him. He felt like a boy again. He wished for a thousand tears more, to have each wiped away by the actress'ś hand.

The director was first to regain his chilly composure. "Tristan," he said in a steady voice, "you've thrown a great scare into the treacherous actress, though ultimately you used nothing but innuendo. I'll readily admit you surprised even me a little. But now that our pulse has returned to normal, you owe us some explanations."

The actress nodded vehemently. "I'll say," she said. "Tristan owes us some explanations! Why for instance does he have the key? Or why did he bring us to this dreadful serpentarium?"

"But above all, when will you finally speak to us about fidelity?" the director added.

"I've been on the subject all along," Tristan defended himself. "You're like schoolchildren: you take in only what's drummed into your heads or spelled out for you on the blackboard. We've no doubt had some excitement in the last few hours: that business with the crystal, the long walk here, my sudden conjuration of the key. Still, you mustn't be deaf if you want to hear fidelity. Its call is weak and sometime it's shrill, not meant for human ears. Then fidelity sounds like a dog-whistle, but nevertheless . . ."

The actress had recovered enough to speak with renewed hostility. "Just don't start beating around the bush again!" she said, casting wary glances at Tristan and the director.

"We've never deliberately beaten around the bush, you slanderous actress, you impudent person," the director responded. "That we're living in exile here is proof of our candor. But I don't intend to accuse you of impudence, since actors are impudent without exception, and singers more impudent still. Whoever's caught in the middle, half singer, half actor, is unforgivably impudent."

She was about to answer the director's insult with a further insult when Tristan, as if in warning, touched the still unlocked panes of the snake terrarium. This time it seemed he really would open them. Again she shrieked, again she rushed to the exit, again the director held her back.

"Do stop your childish bawling!" Tristan barked at the bewildered actress. "Do you really think I'd open the panes? How presumptuously self-centered you are. Has it never occurred to you that the release of these Australian adders would put not only your little girl's life at risk, but mine and the director's as well? Or do you take us for gods?"

The director lapsed into his unrestrained laughter that the actress had known since her arrival at the airport. She hated this laughter because it was like the dread she felt with Tristan and the director. She turned away from it. "I want out, I want to get away from this snake house."

"I feel bathed in sweat in this terrible air," the director said. Tristan smiled indulgently. Once he had secured the small cylindrical lock in front of the adders again, they went past the crocodiles and out of the serpentarium.

"Now you'll surely want to know why I have the key," he said when they finally stood in the cool air outside. "Let me invite you to my favorite bistro. We'll have some mulled wine there and I'll tell you the story of fidelity. Mulled wine will do us good, for tomorrow we may be sick: if we're lucky a bad cold, if we're unlucky pneumonia. It's not healthy to go from the tropical conditions of the serpentarium into the Parisian November."

"It's not healthy," the director echoed.

The actress shuddered at the idea of getting sick. "I can't be sick. I have obligations," she said. At that, Tristan and the director started to roar with laughter. She felt ashamed.

Passing the tall rose bushes on which an occasional blossom still hung, they reached the street and after a short walk, the bistro. They sat down on vinyl-covered chairs. The bistro walls were covered with mirrors in which every movement was infinitely repeated.

"If there were mirrors for spoken words," Tristan thought, "we'd all have gone mad long ago." He ordered mulled wine for all without asking about the actress's and director's wishes. Then he stuck out his pointed tongue as far as it would go. "Excuse me, it's not meant for you, but for these mirrors," he said, his words barely comprehensible because of his extended tongue.

8

"And so I'll tell you about my madness that, coupled with the world's, forms a bulging mediocrity," Tristan said, tapping his fingers on the wooden table top. "Why I took you to see the snakes? It's an embarrassingly human reason. I missed these reptiles, which is understandable after so many years away from them. But I didn't want to go to the serpentarium alone, so I took you along. The director has urged me a hundred times to speak of fidelity. His prompting stirred my longing for the snakes that cannot be true to us human beings. But we mustn't be offended by the beautiful animals' aloofness. A lack of fidelity doesn't always indicate a lack as such." He drank his mulled wine and stared intently at the actress.

"A few weeks ago I flew back to Paris from London." He lost himself in his narration, never taking his eyes off her. "I could see how planes from completely different countries of origin lined up for takeoff, according to a strict law that, since I'm not acquainted with it, struck me as very arbitrary. They wait in a long line, advancing a little each time another plane has taken off. I saw a Boeing from Trans World Airlines, behind it an Aeroflot craft and, in third place, a plane from Saudi Arabia. All were waiting and seemed correlated, only to disperse soon after being airborne, scattering into the most diverse regions of the world and zones of the heart and mind, despite their similar appearance and construction. This shattering possibility – of playing neighbors only to be incredibly separated almost immediately – clearly showed me that fidelity, while possible enough, is inconceivable for all that."

Rattled by Tristan's constant staring, the actress burst out laughing. "Didn't you want to tell us about the snakes?"

He nodded and ordered another round of mulled wine. "I was the snake-keeper," he said after a pause. "I don't know who looks after the snakes these days, but a long time ago I did. In the meantime many snakes have died – I dislike the word 'perished' – but their terraria have the same locks. Yes, I took the key, claiming I'd returned it long before. They believed me and didn't really. I needed the key to feel secure. What lovely deaths it promised and promises me."

The director nodded in agreement. The actress refrained from criticism.

"Since then I've carried the key wherever I go," Tristan continued, "and in the hours of my greatest weariness, I stare at it fixedly, which helps sometimes. Actually I should be in an especially good mood today. After all, I've seen that the key still fits, but that's just what hurts. It only shows how I waste my opportunities. One day the locks will be changed and I'll have wasted the key's possibilities."

Tristan gulped down his mulled wine. The actress, who had not touched her second glass, pushed it to him.

"What made you become a snake-keeper?" the director asked matter-of-factly.

"I'm talking of beautiful possibilities, and you want ancient history!" Tristan laughed, but even this time his laughter rang false. "When I came here I needed a job," he continued. "In an elegant bar one day I got to know Monsieur Chemin. He, so I learned much later, was the king of snakes. We drank Pernod together and so became friends. He gave me a room in his house and for weeks said nothing about his snakes. His wife, the fat Madame Chemin, finally let me in on her husband's occupation. Then, amiably, I called him to account. 'Why, Mr. Chemin, are you keeping the snakes from me?' I asked him. 'I admire your occupation!' He blushed at that, but I don't know whether from embarrassment or anger. He was a refined man. 'My dear Tristan,' he said softly, 'some occupations should not be mentioned for fear of calling death's attention. No acrobat will come along and say, I'm an acrobat, for if he did he'd suffer a fall the next day. I'm a believer in silence,' Mr. Chemin said, 'and only death is loud. Life is absolutely quiet. You see my bald head,' he said then. 'It's no accident. And surely you've noticed my limp, only slight, but a limp nevertheless and no accident. And have you noticed, Tristan, that I'm constantly staring at you? Even that's neither accident nor bad manners. You're no expert. You haven't yet noticed that I'm blind in one eye and have a glass eye in one socket. Yes,' Monsieur Chemin said, 'more than a few parts of my body no longer function.' Then he told me about the snakes. His bald pate, his limping, his missing eye were snake bites, the permanent results of snake bites. Fatal bites only someone like Monsieur Chemin could have survived. He spoke of his mishaps with the nonchalance of a gambler skilled even at losing. His words filled me with compassion, compassion for the snakes the paved world had declared war on. 'If I'm bitten,' he suggested, 'then I've made a mistake. Being bitten is my fault, not the snakes.' 'Maybe,' the king of snakes continued, 'I'll be bitten again today or tomorrow. That will likely be the end of me. My heart's weak, my liver can't take any more infusions of venom. It would be bad for the snakes if I were laid to rest, for who would bother about them then? My wife's heartless, she only takes my money, but she despises my snakes. We extract the snakes' venom to produce serum, to save the lives of people who've been bitten. But for my wife the only thing that counts is the money.'"

The waiter came to the table and again Tristan ordered mulled wine for all. But the director and the actress made a sign of refusal, and so only Tristan received a third glass that, since he had drunk the actress's wine before, was his fourth. "Monsieur Chemin had plenty of money," he continued, "and yet he was an unhappy man. He loved literature excessively. He was writing a novel that he suspected would never be finished.

"Madame Chemin, her husband knew, resembled a prostitute except that she never slept with anyone, since no one would have wanted to sleep with her. She was loud and ugly. She treated her husband as coldly as a cheap whore treats her chance johns. For all that Monsieur and Madame Chemin appeared in company together, probably because she would have found no company without her husband. She wanted nothing but the best. As I've said, he had a lot of money. But his wife poured it down the drain. She demanded everything and he gave in. For his part, he only wanted the snakes. He didn't care about his bank account. Monsieur Chemin was an incredibly modest person."

Tristan emptied his glass, then searched the room with his eyes. The hot spiced wine and his story had brought him into a sweat. He rolled up his sleeves and tore his shirt buttons open.

"You're drunk," the actress said.

He ignored her. "Then one spring day the situation changed. Madame Chemin, who'd gone to Vichy to take the waters, did not return to Paris alone. She showed up in the company of a young Spaniard twenty years her junior. 'This is my friend,' she explained to her husband, 'and he's going to live with us from now on.' The young Spaniard moved into the aging woman's bedroom. At night Monsieur Chemin could hear their cries of love, and not seldom did the young Spaniard run naked through the house. 'A handsome lad,' Mr. Chemin told me, 'and I'd gladly have had him in my own bed. But never would I touch a body that Madame Chemin had sullied.'

"She bought her young lover Cardin suits and an Italian sports car. All at once Monsieur Chemin noticed that he was no longer earning enough. The couple's friends and finally the whole neighborhood delighted in the fantastic story. They called Monsieur Chemin a milksop and his wife a whore. They despised and envied the young Spaniard. Once I rode in Mr. Chemin's car. He drove unconscionably fast. I relished my fear. 'Why don't you step in, why do you let your wife have her way, Monsieur Chemin?' I asked, my eyes closed. – 'I hate whatever's noisy and powerful,' he replied. 'Thus I drive all the faster and so defy my future. When I'm with my snakes, I no longer have serum standing by. I've grown careless. That's my passion. For some time it's been my little vice. I believe in fidelity,' he said, 'but when it can't be helped, infidelity ought to avoid broad gestures.'"

"That day," Tristan said, raising his voice, "I became an assistant on Monsieur Chemin's snake farm. Not wanting to accept my offer at first, he asked, 'Do you love snakes? Doesn't my mutilated body deter you from such work?' I only smiled. Since that wild car ride we looked after the snakes together. We milked the animals – I can recall the swollen fangs, the drops of deadly poison in the gleaming petri dishes."

The waiter inquired after his patrons' wishes and Tristan ordered lime-blossom tea.

"Why are you telling us this story?" the director asked calmly.

"If it made sense and were possible to tell only the endings of stories, ours would be an ideal world. But as it is, we must see our way through everything," Tristan said and then softly asked, "May I finish?"

The actress yawned. "Please do."

"Actually I know only the external details," he went on. "I had to work out the roots and background for myself. Monsieur Chemin didn't even try to do that. 'None of these events,' he once told me, 'is to find a place in my novel. I want to keep it free from all that.' I asked him how he intended to complete his novel if not with experienced reality. But I immediately regretted the question, for he became very sad. He did not answer, but some time later remarked, 'I can't include infidelity in my work if I intend to be true to it. Why did you come to Paris, Tristan?' he asked then. I gave him a number of answers, I rambled on and on, grew increasingly flustered in the process until I turned crimson. He laughed and said, 'We all tumble toward our magnets. When we arrive we're smashed to pieces against the hard attractive surface.' Weeks later, at dawn, a Parisian policeman discovered an illegally parked car, its lights still on. The policeman approached the vehicle and found two people inside, a man and a woman. The woman looked waxen and was wearing a bright red necklace. This, her final adornment, was the bloodshot strangulation mark, and Madame Chemin had been dead several hours. Beside her – no, on top of her in fact, lay her Spanish lover. He was drunk and asleep, his shirt collar open. The tie with which he'd strangled her was still dangling in his hand. Allegedly it was hard to wake him up. He let on that he couldn't remember a thing and allowed himself to be led away without resisting. When two detectives brought Monsieur Chemin the terrible news, he only nodded, and later in the serpentarium he was smiling. 'They've been around for millions of years,' he muttered, pointing at an Australian Death Adder, 'but soon we'll have exterminated them. Then mankind will need no more serum of course. Then I can close shop.'

"Lime-blossom tea makes an ideal nightcap," Tristan said to change the subject. "It relaxes and soothes, it's a gift of nature."

"But how did you wind up in the Jardin des Plantes?" the actress wanted to know.

"It all happened so quickly," he said. "Monsieur Chemin sold his snakes. 'Now that my wife's no longer spending money, I don't have to earn it anymore,' he'd often say. He sent a large number of his snakes to Germany, to the Behring Company. But he gave a small collection of the most beautiful and rarest to the Jardin des Plantes. He was a good man. He made the gift conditional on my looking after the snakes. In other words, I had become one of his snakes: I changed cages. He kept only a single snake, the notorious black mamba, for himself. I remember it well: two yards long, thick around as a child's arm, its bite could kill in minutes. As the weeks went by Monsieur Chemin grew careless. I warned him, he laughed at me: 'Go on, I know all about snakes.' By the time the mamba finally killed him, he was long forgotten in Paris. No headlines in the papers, only a small notice of the mishap. The black mamba was gassed. We'd gladly have taken it for the Jardin des Plantes. Monsieur Chemin is buried at Père Lachaise beside his wife. I didn't attend the funeral. But when I did first come across his grave, I knew I had to quit working at the Jardin des Plantes. I gave notice the same day. I was suddenly trembling and had a mortal fear of snakes."

Tristan began to laugh. "When I think how terribly frightened you were, dear silly presumptive actress, as I unlocked the terrarium, when I recall your screams . . .!" He was shaking with laughter. "You didn't see, you foolish actress, that I was more afraid than you. Your fear was a cheap imitation of mine! I don't even know how I summoned the courage to take you to the reptile house. Never again."

"And then you left for other parts," the director said.

"I left everything behind," Tristan confirmed.

"So I'm the little girl tormented by two older boys!" the actress said.

"No no no!" Tristan said. "Don't you have any idea what I intended with my scene and my story? Are the broadest brush strokes still too subtle for you?"

She did not answer, but handed him a small tissue instead. "Wipe the sweat from your face."

"We'd like to pay!" the director called. As Tristan wiped his face, the director slipped the young waiter two bills and refused the change.

The actress said, "I'll pay my share."

The two men stared at her. Her large breasts were heaving as if propelled by their stares. The tweed of her suit became wide-meshed under Tristan's gaze, opening up and unraveling until there were lattices and fenced areas inside his head and on every fence hung separate checks. The melting pot of Paris had become the director's microscope through which he observed the microbe that insisted, in German, on paying her share. Bad jokes and insults sat as equals at the table, so one no longer needed to invite them, but ought rather to throw them out, push them out of the room with all the authority of someone living in exile. The actress, whom Tristan had resolved to refine and exalt, sat at the table like a shadowy toad.

The two men exchanged glances. Tristan sensed that the day had all been for nought. But the director reached for the bill, looked up the price of a single glass of mulled wine, calculated the service charge and then demanded a very precise sum from her. She opened her purse and worked out the amount coin by coin. She was neither surprised nor insulted, but neither did she sense that it was she who was being insulting. When she had counted the money into the director's palm, he abruptly tossed it into the air. There was a momentary jingling and jangling, a melodious shower of coins.

"What's that supposed to mean?" She received no answer. "Let's go!" she said then. "Evening's approaching. I want to change at the hotel. I've been bored enough for one day. Now I'm looking forward to the night, to people, to the mime. Let's go!" She got up. But Tristan and the director remained in their seats. "Now your madness is turning serious." She turned to Tristan. "You wretched story-teller. You didn't say a thing about fidelity."

"Are you sure, dear actress?" he asked.

Outside it was raining. "There's a full moon," the director said. "The witches will be riding in the night."

9

"We mustn't lose the delicate uniqueness of our relationship," the director told Tristan outside the actress's hotel room when they met to go out for the evening. He had not changed, but still wore his baggy brown corduroy suit. Tristan had decided to wear black, which was not unusual for him except that on this day he wore black shoes, black socks, black trousers, a black shirt, a black tie and a black velvet jacket. Dejected, the actress said, "It looks like you'll be in deepest mourning for yourself tonight, Tristan!"

But he, usually ignoring such sarcasm, replied earnestly, "I think we'll have reason to mourn. You alone, presumptive actress, see the evening as an occasion for joy. We're of a different mind. We have a better idea of what may lie in store for us. That's why our director is paying no tribute to the evening, but wearing his everyday suit and that's why I've draped myself all in black. You alone, actress, want to imitate the bird of paradise. Your dress is shamelessly colorful and transparent."

She had in fact appeared in a long filmy evening gown that glowed and shimmered in countless colors and shades, her bare skin everywhere breaking through the riot of colors. She wore a dark mink stole over her dress.

"Bird of paradise," the director shouted. "Bird of paradise! A lovely name. Tonight we'll call the faithless actress bird of paradise! For the initiate, let the mention of paradise embody the lie, the same false promise that the notion, *actress*, embodies for us." He laughed sensually and ran his hand obscenely over her breasts.

"I'm looking forward to the mime," she said.

As they stepped into the elevator, the director grew somber again. "I lost sight of my responsibilities just now," he reproached himself. "I must admit I lost control this afternoon. At noon, outside the crystal shop, an unwonted fatigue came over me. I don't know what caused it. Until we returned to the hotel I let myself drift. Your talk of snakes, Tristan, troubled me. Yes, I admit it wasn't me who directed you to the Jardin des Plantes, but Tristan, and I tagged along. But now" – he stretched himself – "I'm the director again and you, Tristan, but especially you, my bird of paradise, will act according to my plan."

The actress was about to open her mouth, no doubt wanting to protest her new title, when the elevator doors opened and they were on the ground floor.

"Actually I've only managed to give our presumptive actress a few tiny hints about fidelity," Tristan said. "The decisive tenets are still to come. And yet I can't help feeling that our words will fail miserably compared to what will be said tonight and what still lies ahead of our actress, and of us as well. As you know, director, I rarely attend your gatherings because I can't stand the constant tension among you. Mostly you talk of death then and, even if the group does crave your stories, I can't bear them. And today I'm only joining the group because I must escort our actress. At least I think it's my duty."

They left the warm lobby and had to stand in the cold awhile before a cab bringing guests to the hotel picked them up. There was no doorman to hail cabs. Guests were left to their own devices.

The actress had dressed far too lightly and was freezing.

As they sat in the car, her teeth were still chattering. She tried to be witty. "Have you also directed my teeth to chatter?" she asked the director. Though he did not answer, his silence sounded like a spiteful affirmation.

"We're going to spend the evening in the hotel where Oscar Wilde died," Tristan said to change the subject.

"If only the mime shows up," the actress said.

"I suppose you don't care what people died in which buildings?" he said, but then in the same breath, his short-lived rage turned to melancholy. "Of course not, and how could I expect you to be interested?" he added. "Oddly enough, actors are obsessed with life, whereas poets are oddly obsessed with death."

She tried to enter his train of thought. "And what are mimes obsessed with?"

"Always the same response, always a reference to Sebastian!" the director shouted angrily toward the back where the actress and Tristan sat. "A mime is obsessed with strangling small colorful birds of paradise!"

She cringed as if sentence were being passed on her, and even the startled cabdriver, who understood no German, looked at the man sitting beside him.

Nor was Tristan left unmoved by the director's words. "Please be careful," he urged. "Spoken words clamor to be borne out and we don't want that."

The actress suddenly felt threatened, but did not want to appear meek. "Let him talk," she said, turning to Tristan. "Let him talk, I'm not afraid, because I know the mime." She had not wanted to divulge this secret or more precisely, this hunch. But now that she had blurted it out, now that it was too late to take back her words, she was overwhelmed with questions.

"How is it she knows Sebastian? How could the two have met? How dare she know him?" The questions fell like stones from the director's mouth. Having only a vague idea how important Sebastian was and would be in the director's life and what anxieties perplexed him now, Tristan shrugged to express his ignorance about, above all, his lack of responsibility for the acquaintanceship. And still the director looked at him, sullen as a man disappointed. Instinctively Tristan moved closer to the actress as if wanting to protect her from such excesses.

The director barraged her with questions and Tristan also joined in the cross-examination, but none of the questions led to an answer. In her secret, which stirred far greater curiosity and passion than she could have surmised, the actress, who had felt constantly insulted since her arrival, finally saw an opportunity to exercise power in her turn. Thus she only smiled, so filled with satisfaction that she failed to notice anything ominous in the situation.

Tristan suddenly recalled the minutes before her arrival, when the director had made the apparently casual remark, "The actress won't be needing a return ticket." The director had shouted these or like words at him and now, in the car, Tristan felt compelled to find out what he had meant. Yet in her presence, he could not muster the courage to ask. He resolved to take the director aside and whisper the question to him as soon as they stepped out of the car. But the more he stuck to this resolve, the more monstrous it seemed to become, and when the cab turned onto Rue des Beaux-Arts, he decided to dispense with the question.

The director had become somber and reticent. He had

stopped plying the actress with questions.

The hotel in which Oscar Wilde had died commemorated the fact with a memorial plaque and the building's entire façade was brightly illuminated. The actress tucked her head into the fur. She did not grant the stone tablet a single glance. When they reached the middle of the narrow entrance, Tristan urged her to look up.

"It's no use pointing beauty out to a bird of paradise," the director said. "Her life in Germany, and especially her betrayal of the stage, have clipped her wings so short that all her life she won't be exalted. We want to lift her up, but she makes herself heavy. I dare say," he said, "that she's already pulled the two of us down."

"And I'll drag you even deeper into the abyss!" The actress glanced around smugly and then did look up as Tristan had bidden her. The bold design of the light shaft around which the floors were arranged in ever higher, more dizzying circles did not fail to have an effect. "How unusual," she said.

"An excellent spot for a suicide's leap," Tristan said about this part of the building that seemed to rise skyward.

"Fool!" she said.

"Some of us may reject suicide," the director mumbled.

An ingenious fountain rounded out the hotel entrance. An unseen piano player could be heard over its peaceful splashing. The actress was about to enter the dining room – the maître d' standing in the open doorway approached her to tend to her wishes – when the director shouted from behind, "Stop right there, you blinded actress! Stop right there, actress!"

The command worked. She stopped in her tracks and

blushed because the maître d', who obviously understood German, dropped his inviting gesture and started to grin.

"How dare you speak to me in this manner?" she barked at the director. "I go my *own* way, you unemployed director!" She felt embarrassed in the maître d's presence, and only because of him did she turn loud and assertive. But he only grinned.

"Dear presumptive actress," Tristan said, "we're not going to the restaurant. We've planned something special for tonight. You must come back to the light shaft and then from there we'll go down to the cellar."

Puzzled, she looked at him. The word "cellar" sounded like a joke. She was blinded by the soft, yet brilliant dining room lights that winked invitingly not a dozen yards away, and now she, the celebrated actress, was supposed to submerge into the cellar. "No, I'm going to the restaurant," she said firmly.

"Then we wish you a pleasant lonely evening," Tristan replied softly, "for our group is meeting in the cellar. Who knows, perhaps most of them are already there. Perhaps the mime's already stretched out on velvet cushions."

The reference to the mime sent shivers up her spine. She thought about the instant when, mute and fulfilling, he had penetrated her. She thought about his lithe body. The encounter seemed far in the past. Afterward there had been only horror of snakes and despair over mulled wine, Tristan's and the director's fleshy bodies, and a day without the mime. "I don't love him," she thought, "but there's something stronger, more splendid and deadlier than love once it enslaves us: physical desire." She was not ready for love but certainly for the enslavement. "I wouldn't want to miss him," she said spitefully. "He's a man, and after a day in your company I could use a real man."

The director laughed. "Don't forget what mimes do with birds of paradise," he said, nudging Tristan in the ribs.

"Not only is the cellar beautiful," Tristan said, not reacting to the director's words, "it's also regal." After a pause he added, "Once you're down there, you never want to come up again."

Step by step, in single file they slowly climbed down. Precious oriental vases with dried flowers stood in white niches.

"Scentless mummies," Tristan remarked.

"Decomposition's taken its course," the director said.

The actress had come between them. The director went very slowly ahead of her and Tristan followed behind. The staircase was much too narrow for her to pass one or fall behind the other. She felt trapped and this sensation made it hard to breathe. "Faster, director," she blurted out. "Faster, faster!"

But he did not respond, stopping instead and turning to Tristan and the actress. "I'm standing on one of the last steps," he explained. "Soon we'll be downstairs and no longer alone. We've spent days by ourselves and it's been hell, though a private one. The question whether we're really prepared to share this diabolical experience with human company – I emphatically put this question to you again, Tristan, here on the last steps." He stared coldly past the impatiently trembling actress and at Tristan.

"If we spend another hour together like this we'll all be mad!" she said.

"The rude woman's interrupting our conversation," the

director thundered, and for a brief moment it seemed he was going to punch her. She flinched and squeezed her eyes shut. But when the blow did not fall she looked at him in surprise.

"We've invited the actress to Paris," Tristan said, having considered his answer carefully, "in order to liberate her, to lift her out of her painful condition."

With newfound courage she said, "That's a lie! The *two* of you didn't invite me; Tristan did. I wish I'd never come."

Tristan made a warning sign. "She's right," he said. "At first, it did look as if only the two of us, she and I, were going to meet. But then our formless relationship sought its form, sought the director, and so here on the steps of this hotel, it makes no difference whether I alone or both of us invited the actress. We wanted to exalt her – that's all that matters. But as soon as she arrived at the airport we already knew how she'd resist our good intentions. We didn't have much to go on and so we blindly believed that the actress was an actress. We knew she was flying to us from Germany. But Germany – that's us, and now we ourselves are undergoing the refining process."

"Enough of your expatriate sniveling," she said indignantly. "Back home even the children would laugh at you."

Tristan nodded wisely. "What you wretched people understand by laughter . . . ," he pondered under his breath. "I've never seen anyone laughing back home. My lasting impression of Germany is bickering waiters. And if any of my memories touch on children, my problem is that these children are always being reprimanded. And they no longer resemble children, these small tormented creatures. They wear glasses and have shrill or threatening voices and their faces twitch nervously." He was silent for a few seconds.

"There are exceptions to be sure," he said then, "but they don't even prove the rule. They're like shooting stars. You see them and think someone's dying. But to return to the actress – we felt sure of her as an *actress* and wanted to base the transformation on that. An exaltation toward what is lighter and higher, we thought, should be a stage personality's passion. Then she pulled the universe out from under us by announcing she was no longer an actress but was studying singing with Cavalcanti. My poor director," Tristan sighed, "you're not used to waiting in vain, to being betrayed. No one will whisper of black sails to you when you're too weary to look for yourself. How painful it must have been for you – not to mention me – to hear Cavalcanti's name interjected into your hopes. I loved the actress, I slept with her. Gladly would I have exalted her as my mirror image. I won't sleep with her again. I've come to terms with the Atlantic storms at Finisterre, the finis terrae. Once before I could hardly wait for the black sail to be refuted. Now nothing can destroy me, not even love."

The director stretched out both arms. The actress shrank back from him as she had from the snakes some hours before. Tristan's dark words disturbed her. The director lay his hands on Tristan's shoulders. "I know," he said somberly.

But Tristan's facial muscles suddenly tensed as if he were collecting himself for a great exertion and, almost formally, he said, "We've abandoned our dream of exaltation. That alchemy's dead. What else do we have to lose? The actress disavows herself. We've grown despondent. Yes, director, I think we can forget this trinity of ours. Once we join the group our ties will be broken. Once over the threshold, we'll be alone. We'll hand the presumptive actress over to the guests. She's looking forward to that. She thinks she's an able swimmer, but she may be underestimating the subterranean currents. I wish her luck."

"Let's go," the director said. He had taken his hands from Tristan's shoulders and now continued down the stairs. The actress and Tristan followed. The cellar was a winding passage making a full circle. On the outer circumference were doorways, each drawing the eye into a small room. Some of the doors had been locked with heavy bars. Though furnished with velvet easy chairs and sofas, the rooms brought to mind medieval dungeons or catacombs.

"We've booked the whole cellar for the night," Tristan said. "Each of these rooms is lewd and distinct, but you'll soon get to know the heart of the building, dear presumptive actress." He took the startled woman by her colorful evening gown and pulled her through the winding passage.

"The cells are empty, we're the first," the director said. "I'll wait for the actors here and direct them to their places."

Tristan meanwhile had pushed open the only door not located on the circle's outer wall, but on the inner. He seemed familiar with the room, for he had no trouble finding the hidden light switch. A yellow light lit up the circular room. The fixtures were more opulent than those in the other chambers. A telephone, discreetly tucked away between two wall columns, opened up the world to anyone sitting within the circle. A wooden rack held a small selection of choice wines, and whoever sat down and reached back would touch old books bound in green leather. The room could seat six to eight persons. "Of course there'll be more people than this closet can hold," Tristan explained to the actress, "but not everyone may sit in the center with the director. Even among us there are the small and the insignificant who sit in other rooms, and sometimes the director visits them."

She was afraid to be alone in a cellar with the two men, in her eyes lunatics.

"This cellar is centuries old," he said proudly.

"You talk as if you owned the hotel you're showing me," she said, surprised.

"What does owning mean? What does not owning mean?" He did not give his words the intonation of a question. "We're well beyond such trifles."

She did not understand. Yet not wanting to request an explanation, she merely asked, "Who'll sit with the director?"

"The two of us of course," Tristan cried happily, "and three others. I don't know two of them – he chooses them on impulse – but the third will be Sebastian, the mime."

She breathed a sigh of relief. Then they heard voices and the director's welcome rang through the cellar. "So there you are at last! Rotten bunch of tardy actors!"

"Are actors coming?" the actress asked.

"You mustn't take the director too literally," Tristan reassured her. "We're all actors to him. At the same time it makes no difference what and who one is. Come into my arms, you darling forlorn actress! Grant me a last kiss in farewell!" He pulled her close.

"But . . . ," she wanted to flare up, and he sealed her comedienne's mouth with an almost passionate kiss.

10

"'And I'll gladly leave the movement to you!' I shouted back at the small group, my head stuck out the car window. But I'd already floored it, there were no curves in the area, the motor roared and responded. By the time I'd finished shouting I was already going too fast to risk looking back. The fools that stayed behind certainly hadn't caught my words. I was doing 50 miles an hour, 60, then 100 and that speed called for my undivided attention.

"The Atlantic lay to my left and it was still too early in the day to predict sunshine or rain. Our party had gone on too long once again. The ocean glimmered bright as day beside me. Far out on the horizon heavy clouds hung low over the water. But the light was doing battle with the gray banks. Gradually it became very bright, blinding, and I slowed down to put my sunglasses on. That's the misery of my life, that I'm hopelessly blinded wherever I go. If I tried to see the world more honestly than through my drunkenness, I'd have to admit that my life – approaching and receding – is no different from my sunglasses that filter the facts and their meanings and resolve them into tangible colors.

"The gray was fading only slowly. I felt hungry and thirsty again, but the beach cafés were closed. There simply aren't enough of us to keep cheap shops open around the clock. The lackeys need their sleep, for we exhaust them by day.

"I'd spent another night drinking, without getting drunk of course. My thirst wasn't a result of that – I wasn't hung over – but rather of the plain desire for more. To drink is to become one with the earth.

"I'd spent all night talking about hell, I don't know in what connection. We'd babbled of hell for hours on the terrace, facing the moon's reflection on the ocean. There were no precise sentences, nor have there been for some time. Our positions flickered briefly and extinguished.

"'Do *you* know what hell is?' asked Patricia, a woman you haven't met, and I answered flippantly, 'Yes, I sat on the committee that invented the world.' It was a joke, but no one laughed and so I had to become more concrete. 'It's been a year since I, the mime, have pulled off a good scene.'

"The Atlantic was putrid and spent – only a weak impression of course – and in my perceptions I was deceiving myself and the world. I'm wasting the essence I flatter myself as having. To be a truly great mime, all I'd need is discipline, but I preferred to see people at our parties night after night. So I sank in even the best creatures' filth, for soon there won't be any but the absolute best – such is our boast. One might just manage to blind oneself to his own filth, but the filth of society is deep. The only choice is whether to sink or swim.

"The clouds hung far inland, almost over the road. They were the color of fresh oysters, a touch of green verging on brown and a yellowish gray. The calm Atlantic suddenly threatened and frightened me. The fog persisted. In our country it was much too early for winterly moods. I was a thousand miles from Paris. Something appeared to be warning me that calendar time was no reliable measure.

"Before we broke up, no longer at night and not yet in the morning, our small party had agreed to meet again that evening. We lived only at night and slept away the day. I had also agreed to come back. It was routine and yet more than that, since the few of us are above routine. But then after this strangely oppressive drive through the fog, I developed an aversion for the evening to come. I knew I wouldn't show up. I wouldn't seek excuses. I never wanted to see the dwarves again, not even those I'd known for years and taken for giants. Far too self-absorbed, they surely wouldn't notice my absence. I was justified, I had things to do: I would describe the future, their future, loosen their strange entanglements and so, in gratitude for the crippling, compulsive pleasure I had derived from them, I'd deliver them from their agitation into my splendid immobility. This decision was born in that second when, accelerating and for no apparent reason, I'd called to the bunch, 'And I'll gladly leave the movement to you!' An obviously meaningless sentence no one could have deciphered after such a night of gossip and wine.

"I drove into town and left my car in a parkade. Then I flew here to Paris to work out the program for my upcoming tour. A top mime needs to offer the world something. I'm toying with the idea of miming something unusual, a snake, on my tour."

"A snake! He wants to mime a snake!" the actress shrieked enthusiastically.

"Silence, you treacherous actress!" the director said.

But the mime did not seem to notice these interruptions. In a steady voice that hardly suited his supple body, he continued. "The snake, I believe, puts each of us to shame. Its possible movements encompass the wealth of human feelings. In other words, a snake can always incorporate man, but man can only admire the snake. Because we're incapable of admiration, we fear the snake.

"I reached Paris that same morning, breathless from my failure to grasp the magic of flight. There are two things I could never understand: how two people can sleep together and why planes exist. For my part I never choose either of these absurdities. I let myself be talked into them when I'm weak or tired, or if I'm forced. Last night, for example, when I was finally in Paris again, I was forced. I don't know who overpowered me nor would I recognize the woman again. I know just one thing: I was too exhausted to resist, so the woman could do with me as she wished."

The actress's breathing was labored. Her lips were twitching as if she was on the verge of bellowing something. But she made no sound. Breathing harder and harder, she hung on the mime's words.

"She bamboozled me in a bar. It was my good fortune to be sitting alone in front of a mirror and I was totally absorbed in the beauty of my face. I was admiring my eyes, my lashes and the arch of my regally childlike brow. I moistened my lips with my tongue and when no one was looking, tenderly yet wetly kissed the dry back of my hand. I recalled the years of my boyhood when the director had loved me. That was the time I received the decisive kisses that sculpted me into Sebastian, the mime, who doesn't need anyone or his language. Looking into a mirror alone, I notice how my language is slowly disappearing. Soon I won't be able to speak at all. Then I'll be complete.

"Suddenly she sat beside me. I didn't like her. She put me off because she wasn't boyish. She had wavy reddish hair and her breasts intimidated me. I've always been afraid of them; large ones suggest brutality. She drew her masklike face much too close to my unmasked face. My lips moistened, I felt too naked for words. She said something in a bad French I didn't understand. Then she put one hand on my thigh. I tried to pull in my limbs, mentally imitated a tortoise, but my corporality stood in the way. I was delivered up to her touch. Through the rough and cool linen of my trousers I felt the woman's fingers – no, not just her fingers, but the ridges of her fingers eating into my hairless skin. The hand didn't stay put on my knee, but veered toward my heart. I smiled my transfixed smile, but my face wasn't made up in white. My stoniness still held too much life. All at once the strange woman kissed me, her kiss taking my pulse and breath away. Her mouth was hot, mine dry. She infused me with her saliva. I didn't resist, though I wanted to. I wanted my sex to shrink and shrink, but it grew and grew. I thought about my boyhood, about the German secondary school here in Paris to which my loving director had wanted me transferred. I wanted to be naked in his hands, but it was too late. The woman with the foreign language, the German language, was pressing herself against me, kissing me, fondling me, finding my most intimate parts. I shuddered in disgust and did not say no and did not say a word and felt defenseless and had my hands crossed defensively, but it was less a defense than a surrender of the keys, the magic keys to my body, to the forlorn night. I hate women, I hated even my mother and I hate men too, except that I'm aroused by the male bodies I hate. I love only masturbating over mirrors, not over male and female bodies – no, over mirrors, over mirrors of Venetian glass.

"Then she took me by the hand like a child and led me to

her expensive hotel – rates by the hour or century – where she dragged me into her room. Oh how I'd like to forget that night, but it haunts me and stifles me terribly. The woman ripped off my clothes, I lay naked and weeping on a couch, and suddenly she was undressed too. She passed herself off as a singer, she kept crying, 'We're colleagues!' Her hands with their long painful nails clawed wildly at my boyish testicles suited only for the most tender caresses. The woman took a firm hold of my penis and ruthlessly pulled back the foreskin. I was desperate and weeping. She kissed the tears from my body, icily, hotly kissed my sex and suddenly bent over me. She guided me into her hairy ugliness, I wept and wept, but she panted and raged and shrieked. She pumped me dry as a well and when I was drained and shriveled like a boy, she dressed and then dressed me. I was sobbing, but she said, 'My seducer!' She had the nerve to ask me my name and wanted my address too. She squeezed me hard and kissed me again. I felt like puking. Women violate and destroy us. I staggered blindly out of the room. I made my way home and slept till noon. I hate women, I hate myself. I love only you, director." The mime embraced and kissed the director, who quietly submitted to the caresses.

The actress had been flushing and paling in turn. She reached for the bookshelf and pulled out a green-bound volume, leafing through it absent-mindedly. "It's the same Sebastian," she thought with hatred, "and yet it was a man, not a deviant pantywaist who seduced me last night. No doubt about it" – she stared him – "it's the same Sebastian and yet it's another ... Have you already managed to drive me crazy?"

The question was intended for Tristan and the director.

Tristan was asleep, his breathing even. He was not feigning sleep.

But the director was stroking Sebastian's hair and, in a soothing voice she had never heard him use before, he said, "It's always women who violate men, dear Sebastian. You'll be thirty soon and should know that. A man can't go out alone without being violated. We're not safe even in groups. It's just that most men want to be violated. They wait for it. The male body is made for violation: it bears its fruit on the surface. Any child, and any woman of course, can pluck it like apples. And if we weep afterwards the violators are aroused and happy.

"Even I, beautiful Sebastian, violated you. When you were fourteen. Remember?"

Sebastian nestled against the director. "Speak in the present," he pleaded.

No one paid any attention to the dumbfounded actress.

"We're coming from Saint Cloud. We reach the Avenue de la Grande Armée, then turn onto the Avenue des Champs-Elysées. The morning's agenda is a call on the German secondary school's principal. That's how crazy love makes one! Back home Sebastian would barely have finished primary school – not that he's stupid, but that he loves only his body, which he wants to cultivate and make world-renowned – but here in Paris I want to enroll him in an élite school right away. The *lycée allemand* is attended by diplomats' children, public servants' children, children with a lot of petty ambition. And my little Sebastian also has ambitions, if of a different kind. We're driving along the Champs-Élysées. With my free right hand I open the fly of Sebastian's velvet trousers, search for a tender passage through his underwear and bring the boy's sex to light. How nice of Sebastian's grandmother to entrust me with his education! His penis loves the light of day. It rises hard as steel and twitches in my fingers. If there's a triumphal arch anywhere in the neighborhood, it's here in my car. I couldn't care less about Napoleon's victories recorded in the Arc de Triomphe. Lovelier names can be found in my temple: Sebastian . . .

"Sebastian's enjoying our little game, driving through Paris traffic under the constant threat of being found out. Whatever scruples life in the traditional system might have given him I've removed. His skin is still hairless, his shaft already godlike. But the boy and I are refined: we speak of the penis, we don't say 'prick,' for we despise vulgarities. We? Sebastian's become my creation, he's not just anybody anymore. We're not ashamed to fondle each other on the Champs-Élysées. But we're ashamed to say '*prick*.' Every morality is a morality. What counts is its intellectual base.

"In the Claridge Hotel, which doesn't exist anymore, we walk, we run up to our room. All over Europe it's the same. We travel and travel, the world belongs to us, the twenty-four hours of the day aren't easy for Sebastian. They're certainly not the hours of childhood, as they're not adult hours for me. Am I an adult at all? I was twenty, then forty, and still the question's valid: have I grown up? Maybe I've merely *outgrown* even Sebastian's kisses. He'd do anything for me, pulling away only from my kisses. My breath probably stinks or my teeth are too yellow. In any case we never kiss on the mouth. And why should we? Besides, Sebastian loves only himself.

"I should never have molested him. But if I hadn't molested anyone, what would I have lived for? From whom would I have taken my pleasure? These questions go deeper than our abysmal nights in the Claridge Hotel, than the feigned kiss in front of the *lycée allemand's* principal, that first kiss in years. Why should we have held back? Great events always occur for vague reasons; more obvious ones don't count for much. Even these days we look to one for what we're losing in the other. Since we do nothing but look for what's lost, we might be chided for being stingy and petty, but it's precisely because we're so petty that we're sometimes capable of greatness. I'm so petty I spend a thousand days counting the tiny folds of Sebastian's scrotum. I come up with a different number each time: in London, in Rome, in Davos, in Athens. We never live together clandestinely. We make a show of our obsession in sick Europe. When we've sucked each other dry, we go down to the lounge and order olives and port.

"There are hardly any children left, so only seldom will another boy cross my path. Whichever of us wretches still manages to find a boy prostitute or willing girl is so drained by this pleasure he doesn't go out. And one would do better to lock the children in their rooms, for if anything is stolen these days, then at most it's a boy or a girl, nothing else. We already have all the material goods the world puts at our disposal."

"Enough! I can't take any more!" the actress suddenly cried. "Tristan!" She tugged frantically at the sleeping man's shoulder. "How can you sleep with all these terrible goings-on?"

He woke with a start. He had to catch his bearings, to rediscover where he was, but then he closed his eyes again and tiredly whispered, "Presumptive actress, only we Germans eavesdrop on conversations and then meddle in them. But we're here now, in beautiful Paris. You must learn to shut your ears. As for me, I'm taking a nap."

With that she uttered a barely human sound. She spat at him and, nearly tripping and falling, ran from the cellar chamber and out into the rounded passage.

Shaking their heads, the director and Sebastian momentarily looked after her. Then the mime laid his head on the director's shoulder and dreamily said, "You know what I thought at dawn while driving along the Atlantic shore? I thought: strange how for years I've gazed at the ocean from beaches and ships, always hoping to discover some secret, some insight that would change my life – and how in my stubborn pride I never give up. Facing the ocean, I'm overcome by a sense of strength and of weakness, which are opposite and yet identical feelings. If I keep up my painful search, I thought, I might eventually solve the puzzle of *time*. But then I'll be immortal. When the woman lost control, I felt very close to the solution."

11

When, staggering furiously, the actress had fled into the rounded passage, she ran into the arms of a stranger who must have been part of the director's group. Of course she could only assume this connection. There had been no introductions. With an imperial tone of voice the director had sent the arrivals – mostly younger men and perhaps two or three young women – into various cellar chambers and indeed they had all slunk past him without looking up, like cowed dogs. But no sooner had the director and his guests – the mime, Tristan and the actress; two other seats remained vacant – entered the central room than Sebastian's and the director's caressing and cooing began. Once the mime had advanced his story to the exaggerated lie about his violation, Tristan was already asleep, and never had the actress felt so alone as when she had to listen to this lie. That she was known in her native country was one thing, but beyond that she was also a woman, an attractive mature woman not used to being humiliated.

The man in whose arms she suddenly found herself was large and poorly shaven. She leaned momentarily against him. "You must be the actress," he said. "We all know you from Tristan's stories."

"You speak German!"

"Of course. We all do," the man replied. "All of us have run away from Germany at one time or another," he added more softly, "and our disgraceful inability to run from the language as well keeps us together. It's why we're here."

The actress calmed down. "But what's the mime doing

in your group?" she asked suspiciously and with bitter sarcasm continued, "Apart from the fact that he's in the habit of sleeping with the director."

The man stepped back unexpectedly. "The director isn't in the *habit* of sleeping with anyone." He tried to match her tone of voice. "Nor is he sleeping with one person by way of exception. For a long time now he's slept only with his directorial concept. As for Sebastian, however, he's our group's driving force. Indeed, he's no German, but he's taken his capacity for silence the furthest. We admire Sebastian."

She felt her esteem even for *this* man disintegrate. But she wanted to redeem him with one last question because, superficially at least, he was the kind of man she found attractive. "I don't understand the lot of you," she said. "You pretend to be so resolute and hard. At the same time you're childish and far too emotional. I want to understand you a little, but no one comes to my aid. Especially not your director, who treats me like a little floozy. And Tristan, who was in love with me once and whom I know as an independent, assertive man, has become one of the director's pitiful subjects. Why do you let him run your lives? You're all strong." She stepped toward him, eliminating the distance he had established. "You're intelligent. Why do you obey him? He isn't well, I tell you. I've spent three days with him, not just a few hours, oh no, but from morning till late at night, and I can assure you he's sick. His direction is nothing but idle talk. He doesn't know the first thing about the principles of directing."

As she spoke, he became increasingly anxious. He glanced furtively around him and his confident bearing vanished. "Come, actress, come quickly to our room. I'll introduce you to my friends," he whispered when she finally stopped talking. He pulled her around the passage, nudging her at last through one of the low doorways. The vault was narrower and less sumptuous than the director's central chamber.

At first she saw only eyes in the candlelight, all of them fixed on her. "Though human, they glow like cats' eyes," she thought. Invisible hands pulled her into a softly upholstered corner of the semidark room. No one said a word. Because no one stirred, the candlelight became steady. The skittish light no longer haunted the shadows and the eyes expanded into faces, into human bodies, into a substantial image. "Yet these eyes are ablaze," she thought. "These people are up to something."

"I bring you the actress," the man who had brought her said. "She's not on the director's side as we'd assumed. She says he's sick."

Though no one in the room made any response, it seemed to her that a great astonishment and even greater sense of relief found expression among those present. "I hate the director," she whispered and the six or seven people around her – two young women, the rest men – repeated in quiet unison, "She hates the director."

A younger man sitting beside the actress pushed her an empty glass and filled it with wine. But the other, into whose arms she had stumbled on her flight from the mime and the director, stood in the doorway so he would miss none of the events in the room, while watching the passage at the same time. He was standing guard. Obviously the guests formed no true association at all, but only small factions that feared one another.

"You seem cowed and unhappy," the actress said. "Just why did you come?" She looked questioningly at the circle, but everyone avoided her eyes.

"Why did *you* come," one of the young women asked her.

"To tell the truth, because I wanted to sleep with Sebastian." She laughed, but since no one joined in her laughter, she briefly recounted her chance liaison with the mime and the ugly scene with him not fifteen minutes ago. But even this did not move any of the others to adopt a position. Disappointed, she was about to get up and leave the room when the man sitting beside her grabbed her by the evening gown and pulled her back onto the cushions.

"Stay, don't go, actress," he bade her. And one of the women, who seemed twenty at most, rose from her seat, approached her and kneeled before her. Because of the kneeling woman's loose-fitting dress, the actress saw her naked breasts. Such youth excited the older woman.

"I love your company," she therefore declared a touch too loudly.

The young woman whispered into the actress's ear that she ought to make a pact with the director's enemies. The actress felt her warm breath, felt her own body tingle.

"We need you," the young woman said secretively. "We must prevail. It's not just a question of leaving this cellar never to return. We can't run away from the director. He'd find us, he'd catch up with us. We've allowed him to trap us out of love for our language, but we soon realized that language doesn't concern him. He has no ideals. You have no idea what his real intentions are. Once we can trust you, dear famous actress, we'll let you in on what this group's all about. And then you, too, will see that we need to do away with the director. If he finds out, he'll have us done away with. We're not playacting here; we've sealed our union in blood. Even now, actress, you can no longer step out and imagine yourself free. You came to Paris as a guest, but already you're a captive like the rest of us. Do you want to be held captive? Some of the group, those in the other rooms, want it. But we will liberate ourselves! We'll free you as well, dear, and you'll be our leader." The young woman grazed the actress's burning ear with her lips. "Even now, our bodies are yours. We have no say over our souls anymore. But through our bodies we can regain our souls. Join us, you beautiful actress!"

The actress, who had not understood a thing, felt flattered. She brushed the hair from the woman's brow. "I'm against the director," she declared uncertainly and, more positively, she repeated, "I'm against the director."

Someone called out of the darkness, "The actress is ours!"

She tried to make out his face, but in vain. "I belong to no one," she said. "No one but myself."

The young woman giggled. "No one belongs to himself." She drew closer to the flustered actress. "Surely it would be boring to belong only to oneself." – The actress could see her breasts again and again wanted to touch them. – "Sometimes it's nice to be a slave."

She said nothing in reply. She was surprised that her eyes refused to adjust to the cellar vault's semidarkness, that the shadows seemed to lengthen, not shorten, and that she felt an odd sense of solidarity with these guests. And she asked herself why she had to keep staring at the young woman's breasts. Indeed Cavalcanti, the great singer, was notorious for her lesbian ties and of course Cavalcanti also tried to seduce the actress, her famous singing disciple. Cavalcanti's filmy silk dresses, her lack of underwear – all these little signals had not aroused the actress, but put her off. She sought male seducers, not another woman. Though she had resolved not to give in to Cavalcanti, not to moan in her baldachin bed, she was now staring excitedly at the strange woman's breasts. "Perhaps these breasts mean freedom from the director," she thought. "I've aged these days in Paris. I was young when I came from Germany and have grown old in this city. But this young woman's proof that even youth is possible here. The director and Tristan stink of decay, and they already have the mime in their power. I'll stick with the others who hold greater promise for me."

"Frankly," the actress addressed the group, "I must not let the director take me unawares. You see for yourselves how one of you stands guard in the doorway. I want neither to speak nor to listen under such conditions. If you think my hatred can help your cause, then let us go upstairs. In the beautiful dining room by the splashing fountain and accompanied by piano music, we'll drink champagne in the light and get to know one another. Thus and only thus will I be at your disposal." After the last days' humiliations, she was proud to be the center of attention now.

"We can't afford to go upstairs. It's expensive up there," someone said.

"I'll pay," the actress said.

"If the actress is going to pay, then we'll comply with her wishes," said the man into whose arms she had run earlier. "But we must flee with the utmost caution."

"Who's talking about flight!" she said. "We're free human beings and can go where we like."

The young woman clasped the actress's hands. "You still know so little," she said softly. "You don't understand that we're at the mercy of the director's will. His power over us is great. Not until we take flight will our own powers grow."

Looking disdainfully at the company, the actress was about to interrupt when someone sitting in the dark said, "All walking is a flight. Not until the walk's over can we speak of our freedom. Believe us, worthy actress." He spoke the last phrase with such resignation that she was suddenly moved.

"You poor human beings," she cried out. "I'll leave the choice of words to you, so long as you acknowledge my position. I'm a great actress and a great singer – nearly. I hate the director. Of course I hate him: his ambition is to usurp the actor's genius. But a tyrant's genius is mediocrity. We'll discuss the director's demise upstairs and on my tab. Come on." She turned from the young woman and left the room. The others followed.

As she passed the entrance to the central chamber, she heard the director ask the mime to play a snake. Laughing, the mime replied, "Gladly, but not until the actress is with us again." She climbed up the narrow winding staircase and the others followed.

The actress had become the director.

12

"Paris is an unerotic city. How disappointing," the actress bantered with her party in the expensive hotel restaurant upstairs. "What impresses me most about the city is this splashing fountain," she said.

"That's too bad," said the man into whose arms she had run, "for despite all its melancholy, Paris has a number of pleasures to offer. Above all there's the pleasure of fidelity, but also that of infidelity. Finally there's the pleasure of renouncing your flag and the pleasure of killing."

The maître d' was still smiling in the doorway and occasionally he looked toward the actress.

"Such a variety of pleasures," the young woman said. The actress's other guests remained silent.

A young waiter brought two bottles of Veuve Cliquot. When all the glasses were filled, the actress asked, "What shall we drink to?" She looked inquisitively from face to face, but received no answer. The question intimidated them, which amused and disturbed her. She burst out laughing.

She was about to ask a second time when the man who had spoken out of the dark in the cellar said, "The question must be rephrased. We haven't drunk *to* anything in a long time; we drink *against* things. So what shall we drink against?" The question hit home.

"We'll raise our glasses against the director!" the young woman said.

"And against Sebastian, the mime!" said the man, obviously the small faction's leader, who had picked the actress up in the cellar passage.

"And why against Sebastian?" asked someone who had not spoken before.

"Because he has the advantage over us of being speechless, because we can't express anything without words, whereas he expresses everything without them," the young woman said.

The actress raised her glass. "Against the director, against Sebastian and against Tristan!" She took the first sip and then the others drank.

"Why Tristan?" the young woman asked her. "I thought he was your friend."

She shook her head. "I'm drinking against him because I used to be in love with him."

"I refuse to believe that the actress is capable of love," someone said.

She did not contradict him and the waiter filled the crystal champagne glasses a second time.

"We've lost our reality," the faction leader said abruptly. "Not the faction – we haven't lost it. That wouldn't be an insurmountable problem. But mankind, our slowly waning century, time itself – all have lost their reality." It had become very quiet and the fountain splashed soundlessly as if to exemplify the lost reality. "How can reality be lost, you'll be asking yourselves. After all, it's not a state of innocence, not knowledge that can be lost ... But you're wrong! Reality's a gift. It's conferred on those ages and human beings that live in harmony with their own natures. We're still left our material reality of course – our knives still cut and our pins still prick, our bodies still give us pleasure – but I'm not talking about this palpable reality that's vulgar and does not exalt us."

The actress broke the general silence that prevailed around the single speaker. "Just what do you mean by this dumb notion of *exaltation*? Even Tristan and the director babble about it constantly."

On the other side of the dining room the maître d' was grinning in their direction again.

The faction leader began to speak once more. "Human beings without reality resist being exalted," he said. "Exaltation means a little effort and a lot of the miraculous. Often we need to make no effort ourselves. Someone who loves us can take it upon himself. Yet the miraculous accompanies reality. I've thought about reality a long time, maybe too long. Now I know it but do not have it. Consequently the only pressing question is how to achieve it. Reality *is* exaltation."

The actress was far too removed from these labyrinthian thoughts to follow them. The others sat mutely.

"You meant all the world to Tristan," the young woman suddenly said to her.

"What do you mean?" she asked.

"Did you really feel nothing?"

"No, it was a flirtation," the actress said.

"We've brought some letters for you," the woman said.

"Letters?" She drawled the word.

"Yes, Tristan's. He entrusted them to us once he'd stopped writing them. Now he sees nothing but black sails."

The actress ordered more champagne. "Why do even you mention these black sails?"

"It's an image that's become alien for all of you," said the man who had sat in the cellar's darkness.

"What do you mean, 'all of us?'" the actress asked.

They kept silent. The girl handed her several inscribed pages.

"Read. Read, actress!" the faction leader commanded.

"But I thought you were against Tristan!" she said.

"And so we are," the man said. "Because we've been too close and too alike, we've become adversaries. We and the director want the same thing: to achieve reality. It's just that we rely on different methods."

The actress read and in doing so became a creature of the stage again. She breathed calmly, her breasts rose and fell, she spoke with a lovely clear voice. "Tristan letters, never sent.

"And you let me become so arrogant that nowadays, since you've been gone, I adorn myself with the name, Tristan. I have a perfect right to use it, for I truly loved you. I would still love you now and for all time if I were still alive, but I'm not.

"How do your methods for achieving reality differ?" the actress asked, looking at each faction member assembled around her.

"The director wants the dull system of command-and-obey," the leader said. "We, on the other hand, believe in tenderness or violence."

"I don't understand," she said.

"Read on, read the Tristan letters," the young woman bade.

And the actress read. "Now it's only a question of pursuing our relationship and bringing it to a better conclusion than you had foreseen for us. To begin to write and expire somewhere, just as our union initially befell us and began somewhere. To be with you in the writing, actress, to live and sleep with you and, in the writing, to achieve a necessarily mutual fulfillment. For I've always known we were meant for each other and such knowledge already contains its own death. Rome, Villa Hassler, August.

"Why should I read the letters?" she asked. "You're already familiar with them, they belong to you. Why should I read them?"

The man into whose arms she had run smiled weakly. "There are many reasons to read these letters," he said, "and don't forget, you're an actress. Actors read and act, but that's only a lovely pretext for their nature."

Flattered, the actress read. "'The worst is having to adjust to a world without you, without reality. The dominant impression from my world travels is of the multitude of beautiful human beings, the ease with which most relationships form and break off again, painlessly break. Meanwhile I've come to see clearly that I've become incapable of new encounters. And likely with the least success here in Italy, I'm getting used to the lack of people, which is a different thing from solitude. I turned to Italy because I expected consolation from this country that relates to me in so many ways, much as you, my actress, relate to me or not these days. For I was equally quick to realize that I loved you both. The first day in your presence and I was instantly sure – it was more than intimation or supposition – that I loved you both, you and Italy, and would love you then and for all time. But then came the loss of the echo, the loss of that response everything depends on and on which one must be able to rely. Loss of this response after a happy period, because you no less than Italy – both of you initially reciprocated my love only to withdraw it again little by little, whereupon I only loved you all the more, that is, more desperately. But a desperate love is unhealthy. Only a few can handle it and fewer still endure. I became a burden for you and Italy, I can understand that. It's my fate to grow burdensome, and once I sense it myself I turn clumsy, forget how to kiss, forget how to show affection and finally destroy love itself with my love. As you see, I blame no one, with the possible exception of myself.

"Thus Italy, which I love, became a country in which I'm afraid, in which I cannot sleep and where, each time I return, I feel more disgust than joy. Not even the beauty of Italian youngsters moves me any longer, because I know it corresponds to no inner beauty. My sensuality, once so boundless as you know, has become one that shuns contact, denies compromise and now both exhausts and punishes itself only in occasional daydreams. Yes, I scrape myself raw and bloody on my dreams! I no longer know the meaning of gratification or contentment. Nights with you, actress, were a sure thing at first, then a gamble marred by my fear of being condemned to a cheap scene by you. You rejected me more and more often but couldn't get rid of me, and you knew it, because without you there's neither sex nor the chase. Without you there are no colors. Oh your colorful evening gowns! I'm alone again, and should this solitude stray into a human body, it remains masturbation, signifying nothing.

"You alone are within me and you alone are without, but as I fear for Italy, which I both love and fear because it has lost all dignity, so must I fear for you now. And if it's an agony for me to know you're in Germany, to have no idea how you live these days, then it would surely be even more painful to understand it all. You're no longer a princess and I pray to . . . well, to whom? I pray I'm wrong. Perhaps, I console myself, a relationship, a love, the tension between a man and a woman, cannot be *lived* (I say 'lived,' not 'depicted') except on paper, in letters and books. For it's a question of real life and reality adheres only to the page, not to the world that is round and sets everything into flux. That's why we're separated today, because we slip away from each other, because we slip from this planet we want to live on together. Only pole and counter-pole, dear actress, can offer us security and a home – but poles are far apart.

"We can still hope, but since you've stopped hoping, I must do the work for both of us. Hope: exhausting work for someone called Tristan. Rome, Villa Hassler, September."

"How splendidly the actress reads!" the young woman said.

The actress emptied her champagne glass in one gulp. "More champagne!" she demanded. The young woman refilled her glass.

The actress was intoxicated by her own voice that pushed the text into the background. "The worst, most agonizing thing is that in retrospect I must be ashamed of every hour we spent together, naked and intimate. For me, our couplings were always a surrender and a sharing. But I've done you an injustice with this image of sharing. Was I not the one who took and did you not constantly give? Of course you alone gave yourself to me, abundantly, while I could not give myself to you at all, because I'm ugly on the surface and filthy inside. Using our union as a pretext, I was nothing but a thief of your beauty, one who – excessively – saw himself as someone who gave. How blind I was! Yet now I'm forced to conclude that your submission meant no more, and possibly less than your submission to other men who came before and after me, whereas in my life I overcame my inhibitions only with you and against you, and opened myself to you, the actress. And that is precisely what I shouldn't have done . . .

"Today I clearly see that every hour we spent together was a misery, shattering in our hands. I realize that our hours together meant arousal, fulfillment and happiness only for me, and me alone, while you with all your beauty must have been disgusted by me and my clumsy shows of affection. I was born in Europe. How could Europe teach us to be affectionate? So much constraint and so much blood! You began to reject me, despise me, cheat on me, and that you cheated on me with particularly vulgar people, with lowly stagehands, animals you let devour your nakedness, your perfect beauty blindly – that is my fault too, for through my own nullity as a man, as a beastly seducer – I, Tristan, can seduce only with the intellect and so cannot do it at all – through my long association with you, I have transformed, made regal, destroyed all sense of dignity in you. Not without reason does the rabble kill its kings, dear actress. Now that I've just begun to understand (will I be able to endure a full understanding, I wonder), I add up all the hours and weeks spent with you, like a bookkeeper taking inventory, and I see that public time becomes much less – a murderous realization. Remembering, I covet every hour with you now. I hate myself for every minute spent away from you. It generally seems as if we had always measured in hours, even though we wanted to spend a lifetime together. For a lifetime: how hollow it sounds! But perhaps I'm a deluded pessimist. I hope we both realize that all my absences were against my will, though the realization excuses nothing. Nor can I ask anything more of you, especially not for understanding, since you've stopped loving me and so no longer listen to me. Now that we're separated, I want to see everything between us – through the intensity of my Tristan-longing, but also through some nameless grace that must inhere in so much love and unrequited love – as only just *beginning*, our closeness just arising, growing and becoming infinite . . . Of course I'm overlooking the fact that, in your words, 'it's all over' (whatever that may mean, since nothing begun can be over). The way I see it, everything we ever shared lies shattered, shattered because I never see the facts that are yours, because I'm totally blind to your reality.

"I *had* to disgust you and you *had* to enchant and bewitch me for life, because you're a sensual being and I a spiritual one or, more precisely, because you're a spiritualized sensual being over whom I, the sensual spiritual being, was able to wield power – sadly, sadly for us – for which reason (think of our nights, approximately a hundred nights) I was irritatingly sensual, physically insatiable with you, while you had to reject me, no matter how murderously. For nothing is simpler than to deny who and what we are. It's hard only to be oneself. Now of course neither of us knows who and what he really is. Shouldn't this uncertainty finally reconcile us, dear actress? Cortina, Tai di Cadore, October."

"How dare Tristan mention the two of us in the same breath?" the actress said. Her colorful evening gown crackled and, had she been an animal, her fur would have bristled. "I know who I am," she said, "and these silly letters bore me to death!"

The young woman nestled against her and purred like a velvety kitten. "Read on, you magnificent actress. We're all lulled by your voice. Ignore the letters' content, read them aloud, your voice is the content."

The others nodded and the actress's spirits rose. She read: "We didn't go to the Caffè Greco a second time, nor had we actually been there a first time, since my love for coffee houses always irritated you and since even the loveliest, coziest coffee houses were not spared your ill humor. Such details should have warned me our relationship was impossible. How can anyone presume to create a unity out of countless differences? And yet, with my blind faith in grace, I presumed a happy future for us. But now I sit here alone, a beaten man and yet a victor, because I'm in the Caffè Greco again. I feel at home, dear actress, in a way you never did and Rome, precisely Rome in its suitably shabby way, had already underscored the outrageousness of our wanting to be together that time we came here. We had to – remember? – take separate rooms because we weren't married and at night had to steal to each other furtively, in shame, to defy Rome with our love. Was that sensuality? Naturally my passion would flare up at any time. Yours on the other hand drew you outside, to the Forum Romanum, to the Tiber, out of our association and into another that you found grander and of more consequence: the community of human beings and worldly entanglements that for me was always a smaller community than that between the two of us. You went back to your worldly problems that you call trifles.

"Rome remains the city I love without nostalgia. It still belongs to me alone, for you live in Munich, actress. You do not dispute my claims on Europe. That's precisely why I weep over you, for had you stolen Europe from me a little, at least I'd know you were rich. But as it is you live at the ends of the earth, in Germany, and I'm left only tears of joy and bitter wantonness.

"Lift my spirits, don't send me into the autumn all alone! The waiter in the Caffè Greco understands me very well. He listens to my tale without feeling sorry for me. I tell him: In my Florence, *caro signore*, I'm dizzy with fatigue. I can hardly stay on my feet. Soon I'll collapse for all to see and die for shame over my lost dignity. But he grips me firmly and says: *Si deve soffrire*. And for years he's respectfully called me *maestro*. A master of what, I ask myself . . . . In flight, Rome-Paris, November.

"That's outrageous, it's simply going too far!" the actress said. "I've never been to Rome with that liar."

The faction leader calmed her. "We all know Tristan's a dreamer. He means no harm. He's not lying, but dreaming. Go easy on him. Read on, actress."

The young woman said, "There's just one more letter, you beautiful actress."

"Very well," she said. "By now, it should be obvious to even the most insensitive stranger how possessed I am by autumn, no matter the place or latitude. I have eyes and words only for autumn. "When you, Tristan, say the word *autumn*, your voice is triumphant," someone recently told me. I didn't notice this tone before, but now I pay closer attention to my own voice and it's true: it sounds vain, it sounds painfully conceited in these eulogies and rants against death. Tomorrow's your birthday, dear actress, and my head's filled with plans for the day. I would have gotten even that stupid mink coat somehow, despite all my fear of losing you precisely because of it. But you've abandoned me. I – so it keeps drumming through my head – have done nothing for you. Your birthday will be as dull as any other day. And yet your birth has redeemed the world for a while. The two of us – let's finally admit it – have no talent for celebration . . . . Only a few days ago I had your two splendid pictures framed and I hung them up. Do you still paint, beloved actress? Do you still paint your lovely watercolors that render your suffering permanently and absolve you of everything? Your cypress picture hangs in the room and keeps lamenting the beautiful calm, the enchanted peace I could not give you. Something about me and my name had surely promised you this peace at first.

"You waited, painting, appearing on stage, betraying me. And I'm to blame for everything, your art and your mistakes, you blameless actress . . .

"I'm to blame, a thing I can't live with. Thus my avid desire for autumn, since I anticipate my own death in the death that surrounds me. I want to drift along with the change in nature, with the fading all around me – but we haven't heard the last word on that.

"I've always been alone, even with you, even within you. We both know it, though it's just what you've never understood: that I was content with my solitude so long as you were with me. You, on the other hand, believed you could not be enough for me. But you were always enough. You mean everything to me. Indeed, I betrayed you precisely by trying to feign devotion, since I was too cowardly to tell you I know nothing about devotion. What remains is champagne and bitterness and my icily burning body that grows uglier by the second. But where's the traitor who hoists the black sail?

"Poor Tristan," the actress sighed. "He didn't understand a thing. Our love was a fleeting affair; he wanted it carved in stone. If I'd known at the time I would have behaved more wisely." Her body was suddenly convulsed by sobs and the young woman stroked her hair.

"Why did you want to speak with me?" The actress tried to regain her composure. "You wanted to discuss other matters. What do you have to say about the director, about the group?" Her cheeks regained their natural color. She sat very straight amid the faction. "Speak up or I'm going back to the cellar."

Everyone at the table began to laugh uncontrollably. "Do you want to marvel at the mime's interpretation of a snake?" the young woman asked derisively.

"Or hear again how you violated Sebastian?" the leader added.

"How do you know all that?" the actress asked in alarm.

Her table companions were still laughing. "We know so much," said the man who had sat in the dark. "That's why we want to liberate ourselves from the director, because our knowledge is what forges our chains."

The actress rose from her chair. The maître d' came rushing toward her, a puzzled look on his face. But the actress called to him, "Just stay where you are! I don't need you!"

The leader told the faction, "Relax, the actress has stood up to hear our concerns. We can't keep quiet any longer. All of you stay here and wait for us. Only you," he said to the young woman, "are to come with us. We'll take our friend, the actress, on a journey that will shed light on the future for her. Wait for us, we'll be back soon." Then the three left the dining room and the building in which Oscar Wilde had died. The actress's scent lingered over the table and the fountain splashed indifferently.

13

The man, the actress and the young woman drove through a night filled with embarrassments, the full moon and indifference. Occasional fog banks settled on the gravel road and the man slowed down while the women held their breath and drew closer together. The man said he would go to bed with them later. The woman and the actress laughed at that. As the woman touched the actress, the road became a desolate, infinitely straight one. The actress enjoyed being touched and felt embarrassed at the same time. Quickly she tried to say something to distract her from her trembling, from her presence. Another one, a dream presence, had to be created. Thus, placing her left hand on the man's shoulder, she begged, "Tell us something outrageous!" The man, who could not take his eyes off the road, said, "Your insistence, actress, is out of all proportion to the stories I could tell. My life is wanting in good stories."

"But is it also wanting in history?" she said significantly.

"The director, for one," he replied, bringing his face closer to the windshield, "the director despises all those whose stories are their histories."

"And are you one of these, my friend?" she asked.

"Yes," he said, "I can only relate my history if I'm to tell stories. I'm a boring man."

The actress burst out laughing. "Tell us something that will prove instructive for all!"

"You're embarrassing me, a simple man," the driver said, shying away from her request.

"But I'll never give up," she insisted.

"Very well, I'll tell a story, but keep in mind that I'm relating bourgeois trivia," he said at last. "Before ending up in Paris, I lived in all kinds of places. I was married and my wife was a child. That's why," he said to the young woman, "I brought you along. But I invited the actress to convert her to our cause. Don't interrupt. I'm not telling you my story for its own sake, but to allow the two of you to understand Tristan and the director. You're women and see the world in a different light. But I believe that you're a decisive step ahead of men: you can only hate once you have loved, whereas we men instantly – and on the whole without a thought – lose ourselves in hatred. If we men prove humanity's pettiness, you women prove love's mortality. We're all tainted and only the ocean washes us clean, makes us equals. We should always live by the ocean, using the sea as a mirror or as an image or as a friend or as a challenge. No need to live *on* the ocean like a mariner, but preferably *before* it, facing the fine line where the continent sinks into water. Such a life would be untouched by the losses imposed on us. But I'm digressing. – We've just lost the director. Let's enjoy this illusion, which is our secret plan."

"Which plan is that?" the actress said irritably.

"We won't keep it from you any longer," the man replied. "After all, you're its substance."

"What's that supposed to mean?" she shouted from the back seat. "What have I to do with your plan?"

He spoke calmly. "You'll find out soon enough, you magnificent actress. But first hear my story."

The young woman lay her hand between the actress's breasts. "You needn't be embarrassed. We're women and have nothing to hide from each other."

The actress nodded but still felt pressed. She resolved to ignore the woman's fingers and not take the man's words seriously. "However he exerts himself, his efforts will be in vain," she thought.

Then the man told his story. The road remained a dreadfully straight line that resembled an insidious maze. "I was married to a woman and this woman was a child," he repeated. "But wait – the story I'm going to tell happened so long ago that I am no longer myself. I am another and if I say *I*, it's a lie. It's better if I tell the story differently and repeat the first sentence in altered form." He cleared his throat and drove through a fog bank.

"It's November," the young woman said.

"I hate the cold," the actress said.

"A man was married to a woman and this woman was a child. The two were terribly in love. Their love was confining and stiflingly deep, but husband and wife were not made for each other. The story of their union was so divine only human ruins could be left behind, and so banal the lawyers yawned. The man traveled to every corner of the world and the girl stayed home. She was invited along on his travels, but the invitation was a joke, for the girl had a child. The child was not the husband's, but that of a stranger the girl had met while still a child herself. This stranger had begotten the girl-child with child. The child was born, it was a boy and the boy was blind. No sooner had the blind child come into the world than the stranger began to beat and abuse the girl and the blind son. Finally she ran away with her child and from then on the two lived with the girl's mother, who was a hag. By an odd set of circumstances, the man came to the house of the hag and her lovely daughter.

Right from the outset he felt disdain and hatred for the mother and love and awe for the girl. He also loved the blind child that was still an infant. To free the girl from the hag, but also to escape his own solitude, the man proposed that the girl go away with him. 'But I have a child,' said the girl. 'Your child shall be ours,' said the man. Then the man and the girl and the child drove far away to the sea. For weeks their love was reflected in the blue of the ocean and the blind child suddenly radiated so much light and beauty that it taught the man how to see. Wherever he went, he would announce, 'I've become a father, I have a son.' All the world congratulated him on the indescribably beautiful girl and the luminous child. The child loved the man at once and the girl also loved him, or thought she did. But a girl is not a woman and the passionate nights they shared did not mean she had arrived. The man relaxed, certain he could build his life on this trinity, whereas the girl soon felt like a prisoner. Yet out of love or gratitude, she followed him everywhere. The three traveled through half the world. Each new image of the world filled her with renewed restlessness. She wanted to experience these images on her own. She did not like having to feel grateful.

"When the blind boy reached school age, the girl was still not a woman. She was so beautiful she turned men's heads wherever she went and they coveted her. 'Why,' she asked herself, 'shouldn't I acknowledge this desire? My blind child is eating away at my youth and my husband is years older than I am. He never laughs, he only complains about the world's injustices and he hardly moves and grows uglier by the day.' Twice the man made her pregnant. Twice she had an abortion, for she wanted no child from a man who described her child as his own. She loved and hated the one child and could not bear a second love-hatred. Her mouth grew tenser, her kisses drier. Finally the man disgusted her. From then on they slept in separate bedrooms. They both loved the same works of art, they both yearned for the same countries, they both scorned all the world sometimes, but they could no longer stand each other. They seldom exchanged a word, they yelled at each other and scratched each other's faces. The blind child laughed happily at these battles and loved its mother and father all the more. When the man set out on his travels, he invited the girl along, but these offers hurt her more than slaps in the face, since she was tied down by the child. He sent daily letters and enticing cards from abroad. He wanted to prove his love with this, but only caused her pain.

"Once in mid-spring, the girl became deathly ill. The doctors spent hours wielding their scalpels. The operation was a success. As she recovered, the girl seemed even more beautiful. But she had to take care of herself for a long time and she would have no more children. The thought pained the man even as it gave him satisfaction. The double murder, the two abortions, had been avenged by nature, and the pleasure other men sought from the girl's body would be cold and sterile.

"At one time the man was supposed to meet the girl in London for a holiday together. When he arrived at his usual hotel he did not find the expected letter. He didn't know which plane she would arrive on. He phoned their place in the U.S. No one answered. He called all the airlines that had flights from the U.S. to London, but the girl had not booked a seat on any of them. The man began to tremble. He boarded the next plane to the U.S. The flight took far too long. It was July, and when he finally stepped from the terminal in his home town, the sultry afternoon heat wrapped itself around his anxiety. He let one cab after another go by before finally getting into one. The driver tried to make conversation, the man tried to be quiet. Arriving at his house, he was enveloped by a calm, a wave of silence he would remember all his life. The cab had long driven off. The house windows looked black and menacing. Even before the man went to the door he knew no one was home. He rang repeatedly, but no one opened. He lay his suitcase flat in front of the lifeless house, searched his pockets for the key to the case and opened it. At last, after much groping through soft shirts and silk suits, the man had the house key in his hand. He looked for the small opening in the solid lock that had become a nocturnal shadow. He tried to turn the key, but because it proved impossible, he pulled it out of the keyhole and inserted it again more carefully. But the lock would not open. He was locked out of his own house. He left his suitcase in front of the door and went to inspect the key under the nearest streetlight. The air vibrated with the chirping of crickets and sweat poured from his face. The key appeared undamaged. The man had traveled thousands of miles only to run aground at his own front door.

"A car turned down the street. He could make out his neighbor approaching. He found it repugnant to make contact with him but had no choice. The neighbor stopped as soon as he saw the man approach his car. He stepped out and called, 'Welcome back.' Then he expressed his surprise at the man's early return. 'Where's my child?' the man wanted to know. 'With his grandmother,' the neighbor said.

'Where's my wife?' the man asked. 'She's flown to Europe to meet you. You must have missed each other,' the neighbor said. 'I can't open my front door,' the man said. 'Oh yeah, right,' the neighbor said, 'you couldn't know about that. You were gone too long.' – 'What couldn't I know?' the man asked. 'Your wife had a nephew staying over for some weeks,' the neighbor said. 'Mark, a good-looking man. Soon after he showed up, he lost the key your wife had given him.' – 'I didn't know anything about it, nor do I know any Mark,' the man said in surprise. 'Be that as it may,' the neighbor said, 'your wife had the lock changed because the key didn't turn up.' – 'I see,' the man said, 'but how long has my wife been gone?' – 'I couldn't swear to it,' the neighbor said, 'but it must be a week since she took the boy to his grandmother's to fly to London from there.' She didn't fly to London, the man wanted to tell him, but chose to say nothing. 'How can I get into the house?' he finally asked. The neighbor shrugged. 'I don't know.' – 'Please be good enough to call me a locksmith,' the man requested. 'Come to our place in the meantime,' the neighbor said. 'No,' the man replied, 'I've been sitting in the plane for hours. I'd rather stay out in the open. It's cooling down.' – 'As you wish,' the neighbor said."

"A dumb story," the actress interrupted.

"And a wicked story," the man added.

"Where are we driving?" the young woman asked.

"The destination's not important," he said. "Just pretend you're at the ocean.

"The locksmith came and asked for proof that the man really was the rightful owner of the house. The man showed him all kinds of I.D., the locksmith opened the lock, the man stepped inside. The summer night's sultriness seemed to have fallen from him. He nearly froze in the dry chill of the entrance hall. Though the girl had been gone a week, as the neighbor maintained, the air-conditioning had not been turned off. Each room seemed full of life. This, mixed with an ominous calm, startled him. And never had the house been so clean. The obvious tidiness rendered the house alien to him. He went through the rooms, he went upstairs. It was like a display home. For years the girl had depressed him with her vulgar untidiness, but now his home was so spotless he had the feeling he was not under his own roof. A second tour convinced him that even the furniture was no longer the same. An armchair here, a curtain there, a picture on a certain wall – the house had been altered. The man was suddenly afraid. Doubtless he was alone in the house, but the blind son's absence had dimmed the lights, the girl's absence had turned the very air to stone. Exhausted he sat down on a kitchen chair and stared into space. But in his shock he was deceiving himself, for he had known for some time his marriage was over. He tried to picture the last hour he had spent with his wife, the girl, when she had refused intercourse and then, as he wept, wordlessly gratified him with her fingers. She had hated the game but knew he would be on the plane in an hour. On the way to the airport the blind child had heard the roar of a plane and stretched his hands into the air, at which the man had begun to weep again. He got up and searched the closets and drawers in the house. He found men's clothing that did not belong to him and a photo of the girl and this Mark, certainly no nephew, embracing. The blind child sat at their feet. The man ran from the house. He ran down the dark street and hailed a cab to drive him to the airport. There he went to the parking lot and walked up and down the rows of cars until he found his own. He identified himself at the lot's office, paid the fee and was given the keys. The car was damaged and disgustingly filthy. He drove aimlessly through the starry night. He had lowered the windows on both sides and the draft was a substitute for the affection whores in London, Rome and Rabat had faked for him. 'I'm the most wretched of wretches,' he thought."

"What a pig!" the actress said. "He feels sorry for himself, demands fidelity from his wife and at the same time cheats on her unscrupulously!"

The young woman giggled coldly and nestled warmly against her.

"And you're a hybrid too," the actress told her. "You always seem to take both sides."

The woman replied, "I'm the youngest of our circle."

"As for the story," the actress said to the driver, "I don't want to know how it ends. I'd be sorry if the girl went back to this loathsome man."

"She didn't come back to him," the man said.

"Good," she said.

"But they're living separate and miserable lives and they love each other," he said.

"Sentimentality! I don't want to hear it," the actress said.

The man must have been driving in a large circle. Slowly the fog thinned out, lights lined the road in the suburbs of Paris. "I'll finish the story whether it suits you or not," he said after a long silence. "All at once the man realized he alone was to blame for his misfortune. Even if it had been in his power to be infinitely tender or wary, he would still have lost the girl, because he wasn't cruel."

The young woman was surprised. "I don't understand."

But the man reprimanded her. "You of all people ought to understand our logic, since you've been delegated to explain it to the actress."

"I'm not an actress," the actress said.

"We know," he said. "You're a singer. So much the better: music can not only break hearts, but also bring down walls."

"What are you getting at?" the young woman asked him.

"The moral of the story comes at its end," he said, "and its end is the beginning."

"You know I'm a singer," the actress said to him. "Who told you?"

"No one, but I can tell you that I won't be sleeping with the two of you," the man said.

"That won't hurt us," the woman said.

The actress said nothing.

"The man slowly became a reprobate," he resumed his story. "He promised women a happy future and forgot them after a single night. He could no longer find his way in the order of things he had once lauded. His efforts to reconquer the world step by step grew less frequent. Each effort led to his shaking with laughter. 'When love turns to pain, then pain will be everything once more, love included,' the man thought, 'but *everything* should not be for nought. Even if effort and prayer are futile, at least my anger shouldn't come to nothing. I'll seek out a group. Where there's theater, there's much truth. But where people are merely natural, values are devalued.' The man resolved to plant bombs."

"What did you just say?" the actress asked.

"We're back. There's the Hôtel d'Alsace!" the young woman said happily. "Come, dear actress or singer or whatever, get out!"

"We'll go down into our cellar and drink a bottle or two of good wine," the man said.

"Are you the man in the story?" the actress asked.

"It was an outrageous story. That's all you asked of me and it was easy to deliver," he said softly.

"Were you the man in the story?" she asked a second time.

The man held his tongue. The young woman pulled the actress into the hotel.

The three had a boisterous welcome.

14

"It's always cold in England and your innards freeze. Sometimes a bit of sunshine lets the island burst into emerald bloom, but it has no effect on the cold. We couldn't live in England," said the man sitting in the dark.

"Nor can we live in Germany," another said.

"America's forever closed to us. We could never come to terms with all that space," suggested a third, who had not said anything in the actress's presence before.

"We only dream about Italy and Greece," the young woman said. "We daren't expose ourselves to the warmth lest it melt us."

The faction leader gazed sternly past the others. "But even France has become detached from its people," he said, "and soon we'll have to be content catching at straws."

The actress was surprised by their depressed mood. "Couldn't you cheer up a little?"

At that the leader stepped close to her. "One cold Sunday morning in Arras, in northern France, I was walking through a military cemetery. I saw thousands of white cement crosses and in front of each cross – it was almost November – a stunted rose bush was blooming. How much passion, I thought, was cut short here. These cemeteries aren't really sad, but only dreadfully empty in their abundance of cement crosses and roses. Beside the cemetery, on the way to Calais, was a bistro. Six or seven buses were parked in front, the inn was overcrowded, but not a single tourist crossed the road to view the cemetery. By shunning contact with the thousands who, under their rose bushes, cry out for beer and sandwiches and the living, I thought, these tourists may be more sensitive than I, brazenly strolling through the cemetery. We too, esteemed actress, are not really sad, but only somewhat empty."

She had listened open-mouthed to his statements and the moist soft skin of her lips occasionally flashed in the candlelight.

"Aren't our cellar dens catacombs, and aren't we all really martyrs?" the young woman asked no one in particular.

"You love your body too much," the man in the dark said to her, "and a beautiful body always creates an impression of melancholy and suffering."

The woman laughed.

Then the leader declaimed, "My soul has found a calm shelter, which could be in my belly or even my toes. It does not stir and imparts no kicks, such as pregnant women feel, so they know something's alive inside them. I'd like to test whether anything lives in me or is rotting away."

"The height of luxury is absence of pain," the actress said.

A voice resounded from the entrance. "Where did you dig that sentence up, you depraved actress?"

Not only she, but the entire gathering cringed as the director suddenly stood in the doorway. "You second – no, third-rate bunch of actors!" he said. "Who gave you permission to entertain the actress?"

The faction appeared to become less corporeal and shrink beneath the raging director's words. It lost its three-dimensionality and, in the flickering candlelight, soon resembled a group of fleshless shades. The director seemed to notice this, for he said, quietly and as if to himself, "This ghostly world of shadows. I must read my Dante again."

The faction leader bent toward the actress and whispered into her ear, "Wait for the new day, the magic of morning on which all is dashed."

"Don't talk to the actress, you two-bit extra, you wannabe!" the director tore into him. "And you, bird of paradise, actress, pale creature in the colorful dress – leave this room at once and go back to the center. Tristan's waiting for you. All his life he's been waiting for you in vain, and even now you're refusing to be exalted!"

She wanted to make an insolent reply, but her eyes met his and all at once she felt like a little girl in a party dress, caught doing wrong. Embarrassed, she blushed and was close to tears.

The young woman patted the director's cheeks.

"Always you," he said, evidently calmed. "Whenever important things stand in the balance, you come along and confound the facts."

"Or the dreams," she said.

A sigh of relief arose from the faction.

"We're your faithful actors," the woman continued. "Whether we're second or third-rate, we can't judge for ourselves. You're the director and you call us bad actors, which we humbly accept. But you can't deny our fidelity. It's our principal trait. Because we're faithful, we admire the actress. She refuses to be exalted as we were long ago. She's a splendid example of infidelity. We can only be amazed by her."

The director took another step into the vault. He was looking for an empty seat and the others immediately shifted to make room for him. "Come sit on my lap," he told the young woman, who eagerly complied.

There was nothing violent about the scene; in a way, it was even tender. For the first time the actress realized that the director was a man who could be soft or hard. Without considering the inherent flattery in her words, she found herself saying, "I love the director, because he has a cultivated soul. A pity one can't work with him."

"No one may work with the director," the faction leader replied, "though he works with all the world."

"The director creates the world," the young woman said affectionately.

The actress had to disagree. "Did he create Tristan as well, by chance?" she asked. "I knew Tristan before he and the director had met."

The director said, "You literal-minded actress! I created Tristan no more than I created the world. The notion of creation befuddles your tiny theatrical mind. I'm much rather occupied with constantly giving *form* to the world, and to Tristan as well."

An oppressive silence filled the cellar chamber.

"Give Tristan a form," the actress challenged him after a while.

The director cleared his throat, put his arms around the young woman's hips and in an undertone said, "I'll give him a form."

The actress heard herself gasping for breath.

"Whenever Tristan sees water," the director went on, "he's instantly hungry. On his twenty-fifth birthday, he's standing alone at Travemünde on the Baltic Coast. It's November and there are late-blooming roses at the resort. Since childhood, Tristan has preferred to spend his birthdays alone. He can't stand parties. He loves this Travemünde beach, but he also loves the Elbe River near Blankenese. Otherwise he hates the north. But he's able to see the Mediterranean in any body of water. One flash of blue suffices to let him cross the Ionian Sea he pines for, though without wanting to be there. He doesn't want to be anywhere. He's amazed the roses are still blooming in Travemünde. The day of the dead hasn't swallowed them up. He doesn't want to concede flowers to the north. He, a man of the middle, is dazzled by extremes. He loves hollow notions such as: deep south, far north, endless sea."

"Go on, go on," the man sitting in the dark urged.

"The broad Elbe and the sea give Tristan an absurd craving for cakes and other sweets. He races from the beach promenade into the hotel café. He's pursuing his hunger for sweetness. He orders and cuts up a Black Forest cake. I fail at everything, he tells himself. I'm consumed by longing for company and am alone. I want to live in the south and freely choose to live in the north. I'm my own worst enemy."

"Tristan's also failed with me," the actress insisted.

"He orders a second piece of Black Forest cake, though he's sated and doesn't want to eat another. Still he devours it with disgust, disgust for himself. I must learn to set limits on my life, he says. Everything within me must be simplified, I need internal order. He pays his bill and goes to his Senegal-red car in front of the hotel. He drives to Hamburg via Lübeck. He lives in an attic room in a boarding house. Of course the place is totally inadequate for Tristan and yet he's content with it. All night long as he tries to sleep, he hears the moaning of the chambermaid who shares an adjacent attic room with a man. The moaning arouses him, but beyond that makes him conscious of his solitude."

"He's grown old, he's many generations old," the young woman said.

"He has aged," the actress agreed.

"I, too, want to find people who are right for me at last, Tristan decides formally. Tomorrow I'll ask for an unpaid leave of absence. I want to go back to the U.S."

"He's never had a job," the faction leader interjected.

"It has form all the same," said someone who had so far kept silent.

"Tristan's prepared to quit without notice should his holiday be turned down. He wants finally to be involved with someone, even if it's Death himself. He expects salvation from such contact. Naturally the firm grants him the holiday. He buys books he doesn't read. He goes regularly to a bistro on Milchstrasse. With whom could I stuff myself to death? he asks himself and can think of no one. Then I'll just have to try it on my own."

"That's not the Tristan I know," the actress said.

"His last night in Hamburg turns to gloomy dawn. It's snowing. He really ought to be getting up now and preparing for his journey. At seven he should be calling a cab to take him to the airport. But he loves to lie in bed, defying the time. One last moment in a European bed, and he nods off again. Tristan has no semblance to his poetry, to his legend, by God."

"He's one of us," the young woman said.

"He's become so calm he frightens himself. He expects nothing, he watches for no sailing ship. Tristan goes out often. He stuffs himself and drinks to excess: he wants to become ugly. In this way he eliminates the hope, the threat of being avidly desired again. He knows the little tricks and dodges that will lead him into the night. And so he sits at the gambling table: not every drinker's rewarded with a shot liver; not every glutton's rewarded with a sudden heart attack. Not every insomniac comes to an early end. Still, it's possible."

"Why is Tristan in our circle?" asked the man hidden in the shadows.

"He says, Life is beautiful. No one has loved more beautiful people than he, who was handsome once himself. When he thinks of his youth and sees pictures of himself surrounded by his beauties, he bursts out laughing. He considers it a victory to find the former beauty destroyed."

"Why are you going on so about Tristan?" the young woman asked.

"Indirect jabs at the actress?" the actress said ambiguously.

"No!" the director roared. But then he reverted to a lower key. "Tristan stands for no class, nor does he represent any minority. The world gains nothing by his presence. His life has no meaning for society and so he cannot turn to it for protection. Nowhere is his right to be himself acknowledged. Tristan is a capricious figure. He knows it and makes no demands."

"But we demand a form for him," some of the gathering called in unison.

"He looks at the time again. He's startled because it's almost seven. He hates his dreams like bitter foes: because he dreams, he's achieved nothing in this world. He gets dressed and forbids himself from dreaming ever again. The avenue called Rothenbaumchaussée lies in fog. In the morning darkness hundreds of cars are gliding back and forth, headlights on. A few isolated pedestrians, but only Tristan carries a suitcase. He wants to fly to the U.S. By evening, nothing will have changed in Hamburg, but for him everything will change. A few minutes after waking up, he can still believe in such miracles. At best they're breakfast musings. He finds a cab and reaches the airport."

"Tristan doesn't want to be reminded of his time in the U.S.," the actress said.

"In the U.S. he visits a young woman. She's married and has neglected to forge any ties with her husband. The latter works nonstop and presents his wife with a dreamhouse. Tristan inspects the house, alarmed by so much cleanliness. For him the woman's face becomes a white paste of makeup in which lovely, but motionless brown eyes are set. More a puppet's than a painting's eyes, he thinks. The woman's skin is drawn with boredom. Though the young couple live in the house, it seems uninhabited. The hostess serves Tristan wine in a shot glass. She has to keep refilling it. With her left hand she points out the window to the garage: I have a new Cadillac. Are you happy with it? he inquires politely. I haven't driven it yet, she replies. He finds not a trace of joy in her. I'd like to see the car, he says. At that the woman picks up a hand-sized plastic object and presses a tiny green button. Again she points out the window. Tristan sees the garage door slowly open. The new car becomes visible. The small green button has made the garage door open. He begins to despise the young woman. The hostess leads her guest through the rooms of the house a second time. The two are alone. Everything in the house is new, clean, mediocre.

The wall ornaments, the pictures are unbearable. Seven years of a marriage entered into by children and no child in the house. The husband works fourteen hours a day. His wife does nothing. Tristan and the young woman enter a room. It's a nursery, she says . . . , in case we have guests with children . . . She does not say, in case we ever have a child. He despises her still more. The house is a set on which a play is being acted out. No people live here. The house isn't used for living, but for cleaning. He forces a smile, takes his leave and runs from the bright charnel house."

"Why are you relating your ideas?" the actress asked.

The director pushed the young woman from his lap, got up and laughed as he had done when the actress arrived at the airport. Reluctantly at first, then less and less restrained, the others joined in, and when the entire vault rang with laughter, more laughter resounded from the other cellar chambers. Led by the director, the group laughed and the actress was suddenly afraid. She longed to be in Tristan's arms, expecting to find protection in his sorrow, hoping for his former passions, forgetting the reality of the days in Paris that had offered her nothing but rash anger and anxiety. But Tristan stood pale in the low doorway and said, "I feel as if we'd been in this cellar a thousand years. Don't always laugh, director, but weep for the monstrosity of time!"

"I'm fed up with this game of laughing and weeping!" shouted the director, who had fallen silent at Tristan's words. "And I'm fed up with the game of love." Slowly the last gurgling laughs died down and the cellar was a tomb again.

The actress went to Tristan and nestled against him. He felt her body twitching and was reminded of a fish tossed onto land. He almost put his arm around her neck, but checked himself at the last moment. "Your formulations have nothing to do with me," he told the director.

"You think so?"

The mime came in. His skin-tight clothing drew all eyes to him. "I'm going to mime the snake," Sebastian said resolutely, "here and now. I need light!"

The gathering pushed the tables back and crowded against the walls. In minutes additional candles had been lit and a stage created, which filled the actress with sheer terror.

15

The mime stretched, raised his arms toward the cellar chamber's ceiling, the stony firmament, and placed his palms together. He stood like that before the astonished gathering and did not stir. "It makes no difference," he said softly, "whether a mime who wants to become a snake stands upright or lies on the ground. For snakes don't crawl, but are upright and human beings don't lift themselves up, but crawl. I am the snake." His words silenced the group. Even the director sat still. The actress undressed the mime with her eyes; the tight nylon skin enveloped the audaciously moving man almost invisibly. She felt her flesh crawl, but at the same time was pleasantly aroused by the thought she was supposed to have violated him. She had no precise memories of that night. Maybe Sebastian had not lied, maybe she had been carried away. It would all come out eventually. The mime was truly convincing only when he exposed the truth through his gestures, when he tore falsehood away like a warm blanket from a sleeper's naked body: Don't hide!

He began his routine. Nothing was rehearsed, nor thought through perhaps. Sebastian followed his instincts. His body, which seemed made of countless vertebrae and hidden muscles, began to turn in a circle, the sinuous movement shrinking its natural girth. He changed shape like clay on the potter's wheel. The transformations proceeded so rapidly they made everyone in the room dizzy. Tristan, his head beginning to nod in a strange rhythm, sought a hold. He stared at the actress he had loved once and who offered him no stability now. He felt lonely and stronger for that, and turned his attention to the mime. The latter grew and shrank into a snake, abandoning himself and the world.

While the mime's recital became ever more breathless and gave rise to ever greater breathlessness, the actress noticed a furtive shifting of benches and chairs, so quiet that neither the director nor Tristan noticed it. The group was changing the seating order. The faction leader as well as the young woman and several others were trying to move as close as possible to the actress to whisper something to her. "What will they whisper to me?" she wondered.

The mime, who had now brought his long pointed tongue into play, hissed and contorted his body ever more outrageously.

The actress watched the director, sitting beside Tristan. The two were totally absorbed in the performance. They breathed in the same rhythm as the mime and seemed lost in a trance. Then she sensed that preparations for the whispered conversation were over. Inconspicuously, yet as if according to plan, the faction sat around her. "They have experience in guerilla warfare," she thought. Then she felt the faction leader's arm around her hip. His sleeve exuded warmth. She did not shy away from the contact.

"The mime's teaching us the joys of submission," the man said. The actress shrugged and kept silent. "We won't be able to ignore this lesson," he persisted.

"Why not the joys of exaltation while we're at it?" she mocked.

"Exaltation is submission," the leader said.

The mime now lay flat on the cellar floor. It was hard to follow his movements in the near dark.

"Do you understand the symbolism?" the actress asked

the faction leader.

"There are no symbols here," he replied. "The mime is portraying a snake, the snake's wretched and tormented nature."

"The coupling of snakes surpasses even that of human beings," the young woman said. "Incredible how they coil around and hold themselves. To be naked as a snake and entwined with the beautiful actress – that must be great!"

The actress was pleased with this image, but something compelled her to shatter the lovely dream with words. "Snakes shed their skins," she said, "and their ecstasy falls into shreds."

The young woman cringed.

The mime was stalking prey that he himself was. The lightning speed of his gestures was agonizing. The faction became agitated.

"I hate our world," the faction leader whispered.

"Why?" The actress feigned boredom.

"Having to look at the world tires me," he said, raising his voice.

"Shh!" she hissed in alarm.

"The director's wrath can kill," the young woman said.

"So can we," the man burst out.

"We're not that advanced yet," she said.

"What are you talking about," the actress asked.

The mime slashed the air with his arm so quickly it made a whistling sound. A few cowered as if thunderstruck. A malicious smile lay on the director's lips. Tristan stared at this smile for some time. He did not regard the actress.

"I'm talking about the way the world functions," the faction leader said. "I'm talking about man's need to work.

The countless jobs and their pointless tasks – for what?"

"You want to make do without progress?" the actress asked.

"Yes, I do!" he shouted, so loudly that the mime lost his concentration for a few seconds. He opened his eyes and his movements seemed to flag, but then every nerve in his body tensed again and he immersed himself in the snake's being. It's not easy for a mime to conjure up millions of years in one quick movement, he had said once long ago.

"I'm annoyed," the faction leader went on, "by the stupid efforts people make to keep their houses and hallways clean and bright. I'm annoyed by people's clothing: why such a vast selection in everything? I hate this selection that prevents all dignity."

"It's great to have a choice," the actress said.

"No, it's terrible," the leader said.

Sebastian was miming the hungry snake's attack. To look at him meant to fall prey. The actress turned away. A large hairy spider sat on the grayish-yellow wall.

"It's terrible," the leader repeated. "*One* car, *one* tie, *one* cut of dress would do. Selection wearies me to death."

"You're alone in your worries," she replied.

"He's not alone," the young woman said. "I'm with him."

"The world would be drab," the actress said.

"It would be comprehensible," the faction leader said.

The mime lay twisted over the threshold, devouring his prey.

"He's taking his act too far," the actress said.

"Want to bet that he won't have the courage to take it to the extreme?" the faction leader asked.

"And what might that be?" she wanted to know.

He smiled. "We'll see," he said dreamily.

"Do you know what it means to long for something?" the actress asked after a prolonged silence.

The faction leader flared up. "I know the longing to abandon civilization and go back to nature. People slave to death trying to keep the department store carpets clean and the trains from derailing. They polish and oil and drill and produce – for what?"

The actress wanted to sit up, but slumped instead. "What do you want?" It was hard for her to utter these four words. An overwhelming fear of the question's answer had come over her. She sought the young woman's hand for support.

The mime's flawless white facial make-up was furrowed with sweat now: reddish grooves in a chalky artificiality.

"I want only to crawl on the ground and stammer," the faction leader said. He did not appear to notice the startled and cowering actress. "I want only to stammer," he repeated, "and suicide is perfect only when everyone commits it jointly."

"Who is *everyone*?" the actress asked.

"Mankind," the faction leader said dryly.

The young woman suppressed a giggling fit.

"Because mankind isn't crazy," the actress said, "there's no danger of collective suicide. Do you have another solution?" She felt triumphant; he would have no answer.

His breath stank. She saw that his teeth were pointed and crooked. The man, who appeared stately from a distance, fell apart into minor deformities on closer inspection. The actress wanted nothing to do with the faction leader. And still she held her breath and repeated, "Do you have another solution?"

"Because mankind won't summon the courage to see the absurdity of its order, we must engage in terrorism. That's the other solution: we must engage in terrorism."

She ignored his bad breath. "What's that supposed to mean?"

He placed his abnormally moist hand on the back of hers and made an effort to sound childishly innocent. "Engaging in terrorism, dear actress, means using disruptive symbols to bring about the total destruction desired."

"But that's criminal!" she said.

"Every great artist is a terrorist," the faction leader said. "World stages have always engaged in destruction. We flock to any scene of destruction."

"The mime interprets a snake and destroys all snakes with his performance," the young woman said.

"Whoever produces something also destroys something," whispered the man who sat in the dark some distance away.

"You're trying to legitimize your behavior, but it's still criminal," the actress insisted.

"You're a criminal too, because you act on stage," the young woman said.

The actress was indignant. She turned to Tristan for help, but he was greedily taking in Sebastian's performance. She could not call him to her nor go to him in the packed cellar chamber. It suddenly dawned on her that the cellar vault was *packed*. The director's group had crowded in.

The faction leader began to speak again. So long as the mime's movements were rash, it was safe to speak. "We use disruptive symbols to bring about total destruction," he repeated, "but since we're cognizant beings, we also use disruptive symbols merely as symbols. We terrorize only the stage, mirror of the world."

The young woman grabbed the actress's breasts. "Actress, dear actress, help us in our mission."

"You're mad." Barely able to restrain herself, she still felt an intense desire for physical contact. She resolved to become intimate with the woman. Maybe she could even make the young creature submissive. She wanted to find out why the famed Cavalcanti was always after her, the actress. Maybe sleeping with men was not so important. Maybe a young woman was a substitute for men, or better than that. She leaned toward the woman and kissed her wetly on the ear.

"Be a snake. Don't stop!" The director's voice suddenly rang out. The mime had tired and was showing signs that his performance was coming to an end. His gestures portrayed a snake moving into the infinity of the desert. With his fingers, Sebastian created sand; with his hands and arms, dunes; with his lips, the wind. His body was the snake and only his slightly weary stance signaled the approaching end to the ravenous director. But he did not want to accept the end.

"He's tired," Tristan said.

"Quiet, Tristan!" the director said.

The mime accepted these interruptions with a superior resignation.

The actress was thinking about the atrocities that had for some time been reported in the daily papers. They were always crimes perpetrated in theaters: a bomb in a full house, thirty or forty dead, a fire on opening night, set in ten places at once, poisoned wine sold in the lobby. "Perhaps

I'm on to these crimes," she thought.

Soaking with sweat, the mime lay on the stone floor.

"He'll catch pneumonia," the actress thought. She was surprised how quickly she could switch from major suspicions to minor concerns. "A truly great actress couldn't do that," she went on in her thoughts. And suddenly she was overcome by the devastating realization that she was not *great*, despite her renown in Munich, that she wanted to switch over to singing because she had recognized the all too confining limits of her future in theater and that, as a singer, she might be a clown, good only for cabaret acts. "I'm no Eboli," she thought bitterly, "I'm a housewife with ambitions, nor do I have any right to the young woman." But she wanted her and, confused by all the wine and the mime's satanic movements, she crooked her left ring finger to call the faction leader to her side. First making sure no one else could hear, she whispered, "If it's a question of bombs in theaters, then I'm with you."

The man grinned and amiably pinched her cheek.

"Because we're cognizant beings, we use disruptive symbols only as symbols," she repeated to herself, her lips moving like a hysterical woman's. In less than an hour she had abandoned decades of self-deception and honesty and had changed over from folly to brutality. The director would have commented, "It happens to many," but he knew nothing about it, even though he alone was responsible for the course of the scenes.

"I'll plant bombs," the actress told herself.

16

"Would you plant a bomb?" the actress asked Tristan when they were saying good-night in the hotel.

"What a subject for the early morning!" he cried in dismay, but then added, "It's another question of fidelity. Planting bombs doesn't necessarily make you a criminal. Everyone must hold to some value I suppose. Fidelity toward your homeland strikes me as a very common fidelity, just like that to an established order. Fidelity out of love or gratitude is a few notches higher no doubt. And as for fidelity toward oneself, it's far too Janus-faced to allow for valid statements. You can be true to yourself, actress, and so become a saint. Think of St. Francis of Assisi. But you can also be true to yourself and so be a devil, as was the case with Adolf Hitler. Neither can be denied a certain power. But to describe our modern terrorists, young men and women, as Hitler's offspring is unwarranted. A monster doesn't propagate itself, it's unique. If at this late hour you ask me whether I'd plant a bomb, I can only say: Of course, every form of unchecked violence remains a crime and no end justifies the means. But history also shows us that violence was never used where harmony existed. It's no different from physics. Too much pressure leads to explosions. But physics is linked to metaphysics: a kind of blessing or curse. You live in Germany. We live here, in exile. In Germany, physics has won out, but metaphysics has been neglected. There was no time for it. I tell you, actress, there are parts of this world where no peace can reign. Even the middle ages believed in enchanted places – I almost believe that not just

Germany, but all Europe is such a place. Germany's been blind and this blindness is an unforgivable crime. People are all too quick to forgive for the sake of expedience. But there's probably a higher court. I don't mean God, actress, which would be a preconception. Rather I mean the plane of the intellect that, in its purest form, has no idea of hatred whatsoever. Once this plane is betrayed, events, the dead and language exact their revenge. And if after all that's happened a Johann Sebastian Bach or a Mozart is played – Austria is of course a part of that enchanted world I fled – then I can't help but be convinced that such music doesn't really belong to us anymore. We've forfeited our right to it. You ask what I think of terrorism. It's an expression of blindness and a constant restlessness. Your hands never find any repose, so why should your souls be allowed to rest? If there were no terrorists, there'd be earthquakes or epidemics, and if nature itself grew weary, you'd still be left your hearts. I do love all of you, which is why I can't live with you. I couldn't be a doctor, because my compassion for the suffering would destroy me. That wouldn't do the sick much good. No, dear actress, my name is my small contribution: I am Tristan and I mourn for and because of you. Perhaps mourning is a good beginning." Tristan kissed her brow and slipped away before she could say a single word in reply.

The actress locked the door to her room and threw herself fully clothed onto the bed. No doubt the decision she had made in the course of the evening was the most important one of her life. Because of a single insight and desire, she had chosen to side with crime, and the faction had surely taken this affirmation seriously. She would not be able to withdraw it. In a few minutes the young woman would be knocking at the door as they had arranged in the cellar, and the faction could be relied upon. The actress was afraid of the coming day, but at the same time felt the moist warmth between her thighs swell up: a sea of tender drowsiness. The young woman knocked at the door and she opened it. The woman undressed and the actress followed her lead. The night passed quickly and at last the morning sun fell upon two sleeping children clinging tightly to each other, as if afraid of violence and bombs.

Sleep and death make their peace unconditionally.

When the actress awoke, the young woman was gone. She had left a note: "Be in the cellar at four!" It could only be the cellar where they had first met.

She looked at the time: it was ten a.m. She decided to spend her last day in Paris on a sightseeing tour. She had seen next to nothing of Paris and had had nothing explained to her. She dressed, quickly ate breakfast and had herself driven into town, to the place where the tour was to begin.

The large Cityrama bus was a double-decker and almost all glass. The bargain season of one-day excursions was over, for which reason the bus filled only slowly. The people surrounding the actress spoke various languages. German was not to be heard. Since she mastered no language but her own, she suddenly felt lonely. Paris, the most sociable city in the world according to the travel agencies, found its revenge in the limited horizons of its petty visitors. She looked at her watch. The scheduled departure time had long passed, but still there was no driver or guide to be seen. She grew impatient. She did not have much time. At four o'clock, she wanted to be with the faction at the designated meeting place. "What a fine mess I've gotten myself into," she thought.

At that instant the driver and the city guide stepped into the bus. The driver swung himself behind the large steering wheel. The bus shuddered and its motor sprang to life. The guide seemed large and sullen. He slammed the door shut behind him and turned his back on the tourists. The actress thought she knew him. When he picked up the microphone to greet the visitors, first in French, then in English, the certainty that she had met him before flashed through her mind. The bus drove past the Tuileries gardens. Traffic came to a standstill, an isolated car honked its horn. She regretted sitting so far back, for she was nearsighted and could not see the guide clearly without her glasses. She fumbled for them, then was utterly shocked. It was the director.

"I'm your guide," the director said in German when he had finally finished with the other languages, "and in the next two and a half hours I'll acquaint you with Paris, city of lights."

The actress was taken aback. She noted the irony in his voice when he said, "in the next two and a half hours." She was almost certain he had been friendlier to those tourists who did not speak German. But she was most bewildered by his presence in the bus. "What's he doing as a tour guide?" she asked herself, and the question weighed so heavily on her that she could not enjoy Paris' levity even now. She felt cheated. She wondered how she could lodge a complaint against the director as a guide. But then she realized that this man, her enemy, was doing a proper job and that she would have to accept it, even though she had sworn opposition to him and his system.

The director was the force that not even planters of

bombs could escape. The force was tyrannical and cruel, but it seemed to adhere to an inner design – relentlessly. Indeed, people could set their bombs, but for all that they would not escape the director. They would return to his jurisdiction every time. He was the atmosphere no one can escape alive. This realization tormented the actress. She decided to jump from the bus at a stop light, if necessary, to meet with the faction on time.

Then she calmed down and finally listened to the director's elucidations. Because he kept his eyes to the front, he did not discover the actress. He expounded on the city to the tourists in French and English, seldom in German. Though she knew no foreign language, she used the second hand of her watch to time his performance in the different languages. German fared the worst. He hardly mentioned the pleasant and beautiful side of Paris. Previously, the actress had heard nothing but enticing things about the city, and so had joined Tristan without hesitation. But the director spoke mostly of corpses. As they crossed a bridge over the Seine, he gave the annual count of suicides washed up by the river and, driving across the Place de la Concorde, he talked about the guillotine. He described the process of decapitation in grisly detail, even giving a full account in German this time. When, during a long boring stretch, he invited questions, no one said a word. No one dared ask a thing and the agitated actress, feverishly searching for a provocative question, kept quiet because nothing occurred to her. And so she hated the director even more bitterly. Her only triumph was knowing he was out of work. In Germany, she also knew, he would soon have appeared in front of the stage again.

Meanwhile the city of Paris, dissolving into images in

the bus windows, was shattered by the joyless director's words.

"Do you love Paris too?" an elderly man behind the actress suddenly asked her. She turned, looked long and unabashedly into the stranger's eyes and said, "No, I hate the city." The man did not know what to say of course. Confused, he gazed out the window that his breath fogged up.

At an intersection where the bus had to stop for a particularly long time, the actress looked at her watch. Startled because it was nearly four o'clock, she got up quickly, threw on her coat and ran to the front. Before the director could turn around, she had opened the door.

"The actress!" he shouted, but she was already on the street and, as the glassy bus set off again, she escaped through the endless lines of cars to the sidewalk. At five past four, a cab dropped her off in front of the building in which Oscar Wilde had died, and she ran down the stairs to the cellar.

"You're too late!" the faction leader called to her.

"Too late!" the young woman also called.

The actress blushed. She wanted to relate her experience and the reason for her delay, but the leader would not let her speak.

"Personal reasons don't count here. Ours is a joint venture," he said sternly.

Then the actress understood that she had merely fallen from one order into another. "There's no connection between the director and his group," she thought. "They don't even speak the same language. The director directs in a vacuum and the group terrorizes in a vacuum. Maybe Tristan has made the best choice in his sorrow: he suffers over a lost girl, he isn't desperate for some quest, he sees the world in its long tradition of tears."

She was given her first mission, which involved a large Munich theater to which she had ready access. The faction had decided to destroy it. She was to secure an entrance for their demolitions expert.

The actress began to weep and the leader struck her brutally in the face. The young woman looked on indifferently.

The mime entered the cellar vault.

"Is Sebastian one of you?" the sobbing actress asked.

"He's our demolitions expert," the young woman said.

"You'll go to Munich together," the faction leader said.

17

"For quite a while now I've been living, not *in* time, but *beside* it," the mime said. "It runs after me, catches up, passes me and finally leaves me behind. Each point of this existence outside time causes me the same pain. I couldn't say where I am at any given moment."

The actress shook her head in confusion.

"It's all the same to me whether I plant bombs or not. My heart belongs to the art of mime. It's so exclusive it leaves no room for thoughts of women. I can let the director, whom I hate as the embodiment of our dependence, love me. I have no individual life in this love. The director breathes life into me. It's different with a woman. Even should sexual desire make me want to possess a woman, I feel violated. The violator becomes the violated one: his instincts overwhelm him, he does something he doesn't want to do."

"Those are excuses," she said, "needless attempts to vindicate yourself."

The mime ignored her. With his slender and sinewy fingers he shaped odd creatures in the air, then gazed longingly at their fleeting reality.

"I have to get back to Munich today," she said nervously, "but I don't have a flight ticket. I haven't even made a reservation. I hope there won't be any problems."

He dismissed the possibility. "The return journey's always easiest. When we're really at home somewhere, and only then, we're simply drawn back."

The actress laughed. "I can't rely on being drawn," she said, "for I have to be on stage tomorrow. My time's precious."

The mime suddenly looked so sad as if he were Tristan. "That's what they all say," he whispered, "and all waste their time."

She did not think much of such dismal platitudes. "Will we travel to Munich together?" she asked, "or will you follow later?"

"I'll follow. You'll have to explore the possibilities first," he said.

"But how will I report to you?"

"We'll get in touch with you."

She was content to travel back alone. "Maybe," she thought, "I'll find a way out once I'm there."

She returned to the hotel in the early evening. She quickly packed her bags and was unsettled by a notice in the closet that indicated she should have checked out by noon. "I hope I won't have to pay for an extra day," she thought, but then remembered she was Tristan's guest and that he would have to take care of the bill. Again she grew conscious of the fact that, during all her days in Paris, she and Tristan had not even kissed properly. Paris was a singular disappointment and all his babble about exaltation had only bored her.

The actress dialed Tristan's room. After several rings he answered and his voice suggested he had been asleep. "I'm off," she said, "and would like to talk to you before I go."

A few minutes later he entered her room. He did not come alone, but was accompanied by the director.

"Always together!" she shouted angrily.

Neither of them paid any attention to this cry of displeasure. The director even approached her and said sternly, "The bird of paradise has become a gray dove again. You've already debased yourself by going on a sightseeing tour. Things look bad for you, actress!"

She had known he would mention their encounter. "And they look worse for you," she said calmly, "for you call yourself a director when in truth you're a tour guide."

He stared at her until she turned away.

"I see a difference in social standing between a director and a tour guide," she said, looking down at her feet.

"My dears," Tristan said, "this does seem an ideal moment to make a scene, but even if nearly everyone in Germany has mastered this stunted art, the two of you should be above all that."

The actress took offense. "Germany," she said, "can manage quite well without the likes of you who only run the country down, though they've had nothing to do with it in ages."

Tristan smiled. "I'm not running the country down," he said. "The country is gentle and good, like every country in the world. I'm running the people down, because they make life hard for one another. But don't take it seriously, actress. We're mere puppets and our opinions hang on strings as we do ourselves."

"You've learned the lesson well," she said. "Because the director likens us to puppets, you don't hesitate to call yourself one. Fine, be whatever you like, but count me out!"

The director was cleaning his nails with a small file he had pulled from his pocket. "And you have no manners!" she said, but he made no response.

"In France people sometimes cut off one another's heads," Tristan said, "but then they stick them on again. That is to say, they're obliging and don't hold their fate against each other. In Germany every conversation becomes an effort, and whoever wants to live in peace must constantly put up with injustices. Sure, it's easy even for me to say *yes yes* to someone when I think and feel *no*, and easier still to hold my tongue when I'd prefer to make a speech. But at some point the likes of us must ask ourselves why it's impossible to deal honestly with people. Merely for the sake of peace? Such a peace isn't sweet, but poisoned, and constant bickering presupposes constant immaturity. It's impossible to live in such a country, and that's why we're confronting each other here in Paris. You alone, actress, are going back to the squabbling today. I wish you a pleasant journey."

"You still owe me for the return flight," she said.

The director laughed. "We've been together for so many hours, a thousand years in fact, and we've made no progress at all. We only hurl insults at one another."

"Dear presumptive actress," Tristan said softly, "when I invited you to Paris I didn't send you a return ticket. It was not an oversight, but deliberate."

Feigning boredom, she sat down on the bed. Her childish look of astonishment was also affected.

"I wanted to leave the choice of your return open. Had you grown more beautiful during the years we've spent apart, so I thought, I'd let you fly home first class. If you were the same woman I used to sleep with in Munich, you'd have had to fly home as you came. But should you have been wasting your time and changed for the worse, I thought, one might conclude that time makes no difference to you. So you could just as well take the train to Munich. Had you been receptive to exaltation, you could have traveled in the first-class compartment and maybe even flown. But since you've rejected everything, I'm sending you home in the cheapest way: train, second-class. Too bad there's no third class any more." He pulled a small envelope with coins out of his coat pocket and put it on the bed beside her. "Second class," he said.

The actress sat crimson on the bed. Tristan was lost in silent melancholy. Then she leaped up, threw the envelope with the money to the floor and flung herself at him. He did not defend himself and when she finally let up, collapsing in tears, a bright line of blood trailed across his face. He was bleeding profusely and did not budge.

The director finished cleaning his nails. "Now she's crying again," he said, "but we'll let her cry." He pulled Tristan into the bathroom and dabbed the blood from his face. Tristan said nothing. Not until the flow of blood was staunched and the extent of the scratch wound became apparent did he venture softly, "Strictly speaking, wounds are small blessings. They exalt us and the pain they cause is a small price to pay."

The mime entered the room without knocking. The actress still lay weeping on the floor. He approached her from behind. He had white gloves on. With a nimble movement, he closed his hands around her throat. She cringed and tried to get up from the floor and look her assailant in the face. She only half managed both. There was a rattling in her throat and she flailed her arms in the air, but it seemed as if they had been pulled out of their sockets. When Tristan and the director came out of the bathroom, they stood rooted to the spot and did not interfere. The director wanted to yell at the mime but checked himself because an artist must not be interrupted. Tristan took solace in the thought that the actress would not have to ride second-class through half of Europe now. The dying actress looked at him with strangely white eyes lacking pupils. This look appeared so sincere, yearning and loving that he told her, "I forgive you for what you've done to me." With his left hand he pointed at the scratch wound that parted his face in two.

The mime released his grip.

A red, white and blue actress fell dead to the floor.

Then Sebastian noticed the presence of the other two. He shrugged self-consciously, as if he had just broken a vase. But the director gave him an encouraging sign. "No need to apologize, friend, for without knowing it you've followed my directions."

The mime stared at the two without understanding a word the director was saying. He had been charged by the faction to eliminate the actress because she did not strike the leader as reliable. The leader had asked who wanted to do it, and Sebastian had volunteered because he wanted to avenge his violation. For all that, he knew as little as did the actress about who had forced whom. Only a steamy embrace lingered in the memory.

The mime had listened outside her door before entering, had heard Tristan's and the director's voices and finally the actress's weeping. He thought she had already betrayed the faction's secret and that he had come too late. His tepid desire for revenge had turned to burning hatred. Filled with hatred he had strangled her, and now he did not know what to expect. Perhaps the director already knew everything, perhaps he knew nothing. The mime stood blushing before the two men like an exposed pickpocket.

"You couldn't possibly have ordered the actress murdered," Tristan told the director glumly.

Blood ran from her nostrils.

The director laughed briefly and his laughter sounded like an invalid's cough. "Do you recall her arrival at the airport?" he asked with forced levity. "I told you even then she wouldn't be needing a return ticket."

Tristan shook his head in disgust. "Not everyone wants to die like you or me," he said. "The actress wanted to live. I'm going to call the police. Should I tell them you incited the mime to murder?"

"You can give them any account you like," the director said. "My truth cannot be proven nor can it be refuted. At most my Tristan can cause me some aggravation, he cannot dig my grave. I've been a man of the stage far too long for that."

Tristan knew no fitting response. He kneeled beside the actress. He looked at her a long time and finally closed her eyes.

"With this labor of love, dear Tristan, you're committing the real murder," the mime said gently. "I've only deprived the colorful actress of the invisible air, but with this deed you're sending her into the realm of the shades. There are no more colors for her now. A pity!"

Momentarily Tristan tried to open her eyes, but he encountered a soft unyielding mass.

"Is she getting cold?" the director asked indifferently.

"No, not yet," Tristan replied, "but she doesn't like us anymore." With this sentence he began to weep and after a while the mime and director also wept.

The actress meanwhile slowly did grow cold.

"One of us has murdered the actress!" The mime

blanched.

"Don't," the director said. "Not one of us – we've all murdered her. We're all guilty, but this guilt carries little weight."

Tristan sat down on the bed that still bore the bodily imprint of the actress. "When are we finally going to call the police?" His hands were trembling.

"Why don't we get out of here?" Sebastian was glad the two men did not hesitate to share the murder with him. He had been sure he alone would take the blame, but the two were talking of mutual guilt. They were raising the murder to another level. There, no white-gloved strangler's hands existed, but only astonishment at human potential.

"Sebastian, good fellow, go home," the director demanded in a calm voice.

"And what should I do?" the confused mime wanted to know.

"Dear child, you've never been in this room. Go now!"

Sebastian went out the door like a somnambulist. When he was gone Tristan asked, "Can we trust him?"

The director dismissed the question with a weary gesture. "Of course we can. No one takes him seriously. If he talks, I'll have him committed. Even you are a manikin, Tristan. I'm surrounded by a bunch of manikins." He shuddered in disgust.

The blood in the dead woman's ears was turning crusty and brown. "The color of the earth," Tristan brooded. Louder, he added, "It's my first encounter with a corpse. I'm almost afraid. Help me get over my fear, director."

He, however, was in another realm. "We can choose between hollow words and hollow deeds," he said to himself. "The dead actress lies in front of us. My direction's coming to a head. The script governs the stage. To this very hour, I've remained true to myself."

But Tristan yelled at him, "I'm not playing along anymore. I've had it with your secrets! I'm no murderer! I'm through with you."

His outburst brought the director back into the hotel room. "You're right, Tristan. You won't play along anymore," he said. "My script calls for you to make your exit at this point. You'll drive to the ocean and embark out on a sea cruise. Believe me, friend. I'm the director, I'm not improvising. The actress is first to go: she dies. Then Sebastian disappears: he goes back to the faction. The faction's of no account: it will soon devour itself. You're the last to go, Tristan. Paris isn't healthy for you now. You must go to the sea. You'll book a passage and watch for the black sails. The black sails bode well for you. So go now!"

Tristan stood in the middle of the room between the dead actress and the living director. "Why are you making fun of us?"

"All my life I've taken you, the lot of you, far more seriously than I did myself. Now go and follow my directions."

Tristan still did not move. "You have a great voice, director. Why direct? Why aren't you an actor?"

The director went to the door, opened it and bowed deeply, thus bidding Tristan out of the room. When Tristan finally did go past him and into the corridor, the director said, "You must promise to throw me and my direction overboard on your sea cruise. You have nothing to fear. I'm taking charge of the situation. What a scene!"

Tristan wanted to reply that the director was not to blame for the actress's death, that he only imagined himself to blame. But the thought of a sea cruise allowed him to accept the dead actress and the mad director, and so he said nothing.

When he was finally alone with the dead woman, the director felt as if the weight he had borne for years was now lifted from his shoulders. He bent down to her and stroked her cold rouged cheeks. "I have a great voice," he said to her, then wailed, "Now I've lost even my little circle of extras." He pulled himself together and went to the phone. He lifted the receiver, waited for the hotel operator's voice and had her give him the police. "May I help?" she had asked, but he said no. When the police were on the line, he gave his account in broken French. "Come discreetly," he bade, "so the hotel's reputation won't be damaged. I'll read the paper in the meantime and wait for you."

Ten minutes later there was a loud knock on the door and two men entered. They wore no uniforms, but one of them held a pistol. He holstered it when the director indicated the dead woman with a slight bow. The officers took a quick look around the room and then commanded, "Come along!"

The director smiled amiably. "The fresh air will do me good." Walking down the corridor between them, he saw a whole squad of policemen making for the room in which the actress lay. Such efficiency pleased him.

"If I were a bad director," he said during the cross-examination hours later, "I'd want to bring the actress back to life. But since I'm a good one, maybe the best, I accept her death. She played her part admirably. Some of the credit goes to the director of course."

"We don't care if you're a director or a construction worker. All that interests us is whether you murdered the actress and why," one of the officers said gruffly.

The director found the police methods crude. He played cat-and-mouse with his cross-examiners. And he noticed that this new type of conversation helped his French. It improved his pronunciation and enriched his vocabulary. "If these interrogations last another few weeks," he thought, "I may be able to work on the French stage. The French idea of theater has nothing in common with the German."

He was bothered only a little by the ugliness of his detention cell and did not give his full attention to the cross-examination. In his mind's eye he saw the white splendor of large ships sailing past and regretted he was not a film director. "Stage allusions are more artistic to be sure," he once said to the examining magistrate, "but these days mankind consists of men like you: allusions aren't enough. Perhaps films can still get through to you."

He accepted responsibility for the murder with a polite willingness. The officials however did not believe him. Numerous details pointed to a different culprit. What the police understood least of all was why the director, who had been psychiatrically examined and declared sane and responsible for his actions, would stand by a murderer, why he was prepared to accept a life sentence when he could so easily remove himself from all suspicion. Time and again the director was pressed to reveal the true culprit.

"Why are you being so childish?" he asked at last. "You want a culprit. I'm the culprit. Surely you don't care about the identity of one culprit?"

But the officers always replied, "We don't want a culprit. But justice must run its course."

The director was depressed. The authorities' stupidity was threatening to wreck the beautiful production he had staged. "A proper conclusion, as Shakespeare would have written it, is no longer granted us these days," he lamented.

The faction quietly dissolved.

The mime almost went mad for fear the director might give him away. Though he wanted to leave the country, he stayed, bound to the site of his despair as if by an umbilical cord. But gradually he came to understand that the actress's visit was a story in which only puppets had taken part. He reconciled himself to the idea that he had followed orders and so acted blamelessly. "I'm a somebody again," he thought.

Weeks later the director was finally sentenced to life imprisonment. He would have preferred the guillotine, but the judges had grown sparing in its use.

And so the director made his exit without drama or poetry.

Tristan took his advice. His driving ambition was to find a black sail, a black sail appearing on the horizon.

18

"I dominate the ocean and so the world," Tristan thought as he sat on a terrace high above the harbor. He called the waiter and paid for his campari. Then he went down to the harbor and boarded a small boat that ferried him to the ship. The water in the bay was painfully clear, every stone on the bottom visible. The large ship lay anchored far from shore and was pitching in invisible winds and currents. From the inn's terrace Tristan had closely observed this motion. He had seen the ship from every possible angle and now he was eager to board the white colossus that became more and more dazzling as they approached. At last the ferry-boat lay alongside. From the bulwarks hung a wooden staircase by which Tristan boarded the ship. A young sailor in white uniform led him to the purser's office. There Tristan showed his papers and was issued his cabin number. Then another man in white uniform took him to the cabin. Tristan tipped the steward, then locked himself in and pinched his eyes shut.

"Not until I can tell that I'm aboard a ship, even in the dark," he thought, "will I have earned the right to be here." Mentally he replayed the recent events and realized he had in fact boarded this ship as a fugitive. And yet he was not running away from anything, since his conscience was clear.

An agreeable fatigue spread through him. No evil deed would exact its revenge. The oceans of the world do not pay anything back in kind. They are neither endless nor temperamental. "We load the ships with goods and people and ply the ocean with words," he mumbled.

He left the cabin and went to the upper deck.

When the ship weighed anchor, its stern shaken by the engines' pitching and rolling, Tristan enjoyed the broken calm. He could endure genuine peace only for brief periods.

The sun was at its zenith. Walking forward and aft along the upper deck, he tried to position himself exactly beneath. He wanted his shadow to coincide with his real body and disappear inside it. Then, he thought, he would be a luminary, if lacking a soul: a wretched Peter Schlemihl. But the sun turned aside and filtered toward the water. Tristan could not keep up.

He took a deck chair and positioned it right on the bow. The wind blew too forcefully against the ship, against Tristan, to be agreeable. He sat down in his chair. Now he saw only water and, blurring because it was so close, the white steel railing. On the foremost edge of the ship, he flattered himself as being ahead of everyone else aboard and in fact, ahead of the ship itself.

Calm and rested, Tristan sat in the wind and was happy. The ship, more than a hundred yards long, lay behind him as if dissolved. "And so I've turned this colossal ship into my living quarters," he thought and, turning to the ocean, added, "Your power is great, but mine is greater."

Thus Tristan, who had longed to be alone, had entered into conversation with the sea on the very first day of his cruise. No answer was forthcoming to be sure, but it was a dialogue nevertheless.

He wore the white linen trousers he had bought in Rome years ago. Looking down at them he suddenly found the slight curvature of his thighs arousing. For a moment he tried to suppress it, but then he let himself be gently carried away. "Now I've become like the ocean," he said under his breath, "in love with no one but myself."

He smiled in bewilderment, then slapped his thighs till it hurt. He became fully conscious again. "What the hell! The ocean isn't in love with itself, the ocean is the ocean."

He got up from the deck chair and, suddenly dead tired, dragged himself along the portside railing to the stern. When he reached it, he felt an all too ridiculous sense of satisfaction. "I can still keep my madness in check," he reflected, "and yet I slip into it ever more unconsciously. It's like falling into water, except that I know how to swim and so save myself each time. But maybe the current will carry me off before long. And still it's lovely to slowly go mad: it has its own rhythm; madness accords well with the world." He felt out of breath and gasped for air. "Even walking from bow to stern gives me a sense of accomplishment. I've made an about-face and for all that everything remains as it was. You, ocean – I wish I could caress you."

Tristan needed the cruise to straighten himself out mentally. In fact he should have lived aboard a ship permanently. It would have been good for his troubled relations with the world. But who spends all his time aboard a ship? So much security is not granted one.

Mentally Tristan composed a letter to the actress, his actress, lover and foe, who had one day died on him, who had only *been* everything, who never stayed put in the present. He wrote, he repeated himself, in a hurried mental script he laid himself bare.

"Beloved, today I'm suffering an agony of longing for you. Every pale and beautiful person brings me to tears. I think of your perfect body, which it's my right to possess, since I still grieve over you even today. I look down at my linen trousers and think of your precious face that I likewise have a right to kiss, since my head is filled with the loveliest thoughts about you. Trade me your outer for my inner self, and forgive me my self-confidence that I need to survive. Someone must survive you after all. I love you, my actress. For me no other woman exists: spiritual ties with you and no other, sexual union with you and no other. The thought kills me that you give your perfect body to other men, animals all! I am Tristan, the man for you, and the stars and the sea belong to me. I want to penetrate you, bore so deeply into you that you'll cry out with passion once more as at the beginning. But I don't want to spend my Tristan seed inside you – it would only beget further sorrow – but rather fill you with love, with regret and with love, so you'll come back to me. I know I've tossed these phrases at you a hundred times before, but not even an infinite number would suffice. I'm aboard the ship, actress, and easy to reach. And I'm leading a chaste life. It's been centuries since I've been inside you. This knowledge is the cancer that devours me. My beloved actress, I know I'm on fire, that any contact with me was terrible and would be again. Still I'm proud of myself and of you and of us. According to a higher law we're innocent."

Tristan stopped. "Good taste before truth and feeling," he said aloud and he found his sentences were becoming extremely convoluted again. "Keep it simple, straightforward," the director had always insisted. "Everything's to become simpler, including my language," Tristan said. "Even the sea cruise will serve for that."

Stars had appeared in the sky. A boy with a Canadian maple leaf on his windbreaker was leaning on the railing some distance from Tristan. He was twelve or thirteen. Tristan wanted to address the child, but the cruise had made him shy. Waves and stars were making him tongue-tied. "Now I'm in the same position as the actress," he thought wearily. He was clearing his throat, trying to cough his vocal cords into working order, when the boy approached him and said, "Excuse me, sir, do you speak English?" Tristan looked up and gave a start. The boy's hair was soft and wavy as a girl's and in his face was a sorrow that, combined with his own, would have to turn the world upside-down. Staring at the child, he could summon enough strength only for a curt "Yes."

"Do you know the names of the stars?" the boy asked and Tristan, who would rather have been asking the questions himself, was forced to abandon his curiosity.

The boy listened to the night and then said, "I'm interested in the universe." Whenever Tristan fell silent, the child would point his slender hand at another star. The gesture was all the more touching for Tristan because a temporary bridge was formed between the small pointing hand and the infinitely large, infinitely distant light, an unmistakably clear line that revealed something of the power of the spirit and delighted him.

"Sea cruises serve even for that," Tristan said. "They bring the stars closer and let one meet people like you."

"Yes," the boy said.

Love for a boy, Tristan thought, must be the most beautiful, purest thing life has to offer. But unfortunately such a love is impossible.

Then a voice out of the darkness summoned the child, and he departed without another word.

Tristan knew he would not see him again.

Now he was alone beneath the stars. He would gladly have heard music to dispel his somber thoughts, but there was no music on the outer deck. "On difficult days I wallow in Beethoven's Spring Sonata. How much consolation the solitude of the deceased can still provide," he thought. "But on the ocean, everything is consolation. There is no human consolation."

Now he found time to reflect on the past hours of his sea journey. Nothing had been tangible except for the radiant sun that does not permit one to look at it. He could recall the zenith shadow-play, but Tristan had missed the twilight, the world's turning gray, the rich shades of the fading process. "The transitions on cruises are harsh," he assured himself. "At sea we lose our sense for subtle shades. Someone who's lived at sea a long time must surely turn frightfully crass. The deep lines in old sailors' faces are passages into their souls: all they can do is live in the currents. Subdued evening sketches belong to the inoffensive land. The apocalyptic evening sun," Tristan mumbled. "Why is the most familiar threat always contained in that alien beauty?"

He moved his hands probingly and with care. He wanted to take the low evening sun in the west into his hands and warm it. Each day he grew brasher in his faith in cosmic excesses.

Tristan was cold. "I want to sleep now," he said into the emptiness, "but not even the longest and deepest sleep can refresh me any longer. I sleep and wake up tired as before. So gradually my head alone rules over me – a poor monarch. And the laws of nature no longer apply."

A man hidden in Tristan's immediate vicinity laughed

and called out of the dark, "Are you so lonely, you funny man, that you need to talk to yourself? What is it you've done with human beings?"

Embarrassed for having talked to himself, Tristan did not reply. He ran off. "And so even sea cruises end in flight and ugliness," he thought when, out of breath, he reached his cabin and locked the door behind him. He stretched out on his bed and slowly calmed down. Before long his heart was beating normally again and his breath came rhythmically. Tenderly he kissed the white pillow of his bed. It occurred to him how such sea cruises can only give intimations of everything without signifying anything, how inconceivably they dissolve life and its memories into nothing. Then he fell asleep. Sleeping, he dreamed of the actress, and the ship left the land far behind.

Excerpts from reviews:

Black Sails [is] a work of macabre pithiness, written in a sort of prose rarely encountered nowadays, a mixture of E.T.A. Hoffmann, Oscar Wilde, and Beckett. Skwara is a dialectician in the sense that the romanticists were – from Ludwig Tieck, for whom the horse rides the rider, to Karl Marx, the greatest romanticist of all.

The characters who inhabit the novel have no names; in Skwara's poetic work identities are interchangeable and a truth exists only to be refuted by another truth. So it is hopeless to try to define the characters ideologically. They remain figures in an intellectual game, in which each participant is exposed to an intellectual demolition test taking place on an imaginary stage.

The characters are: the actress, the director, the pantomimist, and a man by the name of Tristan, in whom the reader most likely recognizes the author himself. Their existences are not externally determined but are conjured up by Skwara's linguistic imaginativeness, by his delight in rhetorical adventure, in lexical pleasure, in the aperçu. What links these people is the power they exert over others, their susceptibility to either dominate or to be dominated – in short, that drama of interpersonal relationships that has no real content but arises from the fact that people with different intentions and interests come together and bump into one another.

To be sure, something else happens in the novel. At the director's order, the pantomimist murders the actress. It could be the other way around, though and this would still be a splendid book. For Skwara is a master of language. He is endowed with the gift of the genuine narrator to compel the reader's belief, to incite his or her curiosity about the creative escapades of his linguistic art. Precisely because Skwara's figures move like marionettes on the strings of his lexical art, this latter is the real content of his book and what makes it a literary event. Skwara writes German in which the familiar exerts a mysterious new effect, unfathomable and legendlike. He thereby complies with Kandinsky's demand at the fin de siècle that art must again be mysterious.

Hans Sahl in *Die Welt*

[This novel] embodies a thesis that will doubtless produce a reactionary effect in the minds of socially engaged authors and readers: the precedence of the poetic project over real life. Form precedes material. Art is not live performance.

K. H. Kramberg in *Süddeutsche Zeitung*